"If you live to be a hundred you might never see anything half as beautiful as this."

Northern lights. She let out a gasp as a myriad of colors undulated across the sky. Greens. White. A splash of red appeared. Violet streaks of light shimmered across the sky.

She tilted her head back and stared up at the heavens in wonder. "How is this happening?"

Boone's explanation came swiftly. "It's a storm of sorts. The effect comes from directional changes in the earth's magnetic field. Our ancestors theorized it was past and future events being displayed across the sky."

She raised her hand toward the vibrating lights. It felt as if she might be able to reach out and grab hold of the bright, flashing waves.

"It's magnificent," she said. It was almost as if a painter had made the sky their canvas and splashed paint all over the heavens.

"Beautiful," Boone said with a sigh.

When she turned toward him, his eyes ~~were~~ focused solely on ~~her~~ ~~instead of~~ the aurora boreali~~s.~~

Belle Calhoune grew up in a small town in Massachusetts. Married to her college sweetheart, she is raising two lovely daughters in Connecticut. A dog lover, she has one mini poodle and a chocolate Lab. Writing for the Love Inspired line is a dream come true. Working at home in her pajamas is one of the best perks of the job. Belle enjoys summers in Cape Cod, traveling and reading.

Books by Belle Calhoune

Love Inspired

An Alaskan Wedding

Belle Calhoune

Recycling programs
for this product may
not exist in your area.

LOVE INSPIRED BOOKS

ISBN-13: 978-0-373-87983-0

An Alaskan Wedding

www.Harlequin.com

Printed in U.S.A.

This is love: that we walk in obedience to God's commands. As you have heard from the beginning His command is that you walk in love.

—*2 John* 1:6

To my sister, Karen.
You were my very first fan. And for many years,
my only fan. Thank you for cheering me on
and for always believing in the dream.

Acknowledgments

For my family: Randy, Sierra and Amber.
Thanks for understanding that writing
is a vital part of my life and for celebrating
all my joyful news.

For my editor, Emily Rodmell, for your
continued support, wisdom and vision.

For the Jack and Jill Moms, Stamford-Norwalk.
You guys rock!!!
Thanks for always celebrating me.

To all the readers of the Love Inspired line. I so
appreciate your enthusiasm and encouragement,
as well as your heartfelt letters.

Chapter One

◟◞

Grace Corbett peered out the window of the seaplane, her eyes sweeping over a craggy landscape that looked as if it came straight out of an Alaskan postcard. Majestic white-capped mountains loomed in the distance. A wide expanse of tundra stretched out for miles. Vibrant, green trees dusted with snow dotted the scenery. Firs, spruce and pines, she imagined. She'd done a lot of reading in the past few weeks about Alaska in preparation for her assignment for the *New York Tribune*. According to her literature, these types of trees were among the most abundant found in the state.

The plane was preparing for its final descent over Kachemak Bay, and it was proving to be a bumpy ride. The bucking motion of the plane was giving her motion sickness. She tried taking slow, shallow breaths to calm herself. "Focus on the moment, not the panic," she whispered, reciting the mantra from her fear-of-flying class. "You're here. You're alive. You're here. You're alive," she chanted.

"Poor thing. You look terrified." The Southern twang pierced through her terror, reminding her that she wasn't the only passenger on the flight to Love. She turned to the woman seated next to her, making eye contact with the attractive redhead who was staring at her with a look that oozed sympathy. Although she could tell from her expression the woman was well-meaning, it irritated Grace to be the object of someone's pity. Been there, done that, she thought grumpily. She'd long ago decided that even if she lived to be one hundred and ten, no one was allowed to host a pity party in her honor. Even if it killed her, she was going to hold her head up high. Her chin trembled as she nodded. "I—I don't like planes. Especially little ones."

She let out a moan as the plane bucked and shuddered, jerking her to and fro. Nausea rose up in her throat. Raising a hand to her mouth, she uttered a silent prayer to the big guy upstairs. Even though she'd desperately wanted this assignment, being stuck on a tin-can plane hadn't been part of the bargain. Something told her that her boss Tony hadn't wanted her to know before she got to Anchorage about the so-called plane she'd be flying on for the last leg of her journey.

The Southern twang intruded on her thoughts again. "I guess you're not a good flier. You're as pale as a sheet," she said with a knowing look. "I'm Sophie Miller from Saskell, Georgia." She reached out and clutched Grace's hand. "Hold my hand, darlin'. Squeeze it as hard as you like. I won't flinch."

Grace obeyed without question, tightly squeezing Sophie's hand. Strangely enough, it made her feel better. If the plane was going down, at least she wouldn't be alone.

"I'm G-Grace, from New York City. Grace Corbett." Fear was making her teeth chatter uncontrollably. The sound of it rattled in her ears above the roar of the plane.

"Nice to meet you, Grace," Sophie said with a grin "I'm so excited about this adventure we're embarking on," she gushed. "Taking a job in an Alaskan fishing village. Talk about a leap of faith."

Grace sighed. "Yeah, it's a real leap of faith." She knew exactly what Sophie was talking about. Love. It was the reason she'd flown ten hours from New York to reach the remote town of Love, Alaska. It was all due to the pursuit of love. And happiness. *And white picket fences covered in ice crystals and snow*, she thought crankily.

If only she wasn't such a cynic about happily-ever-after. If only she wasn't so deathly afraid of planes. And spiders. And being led astray by her feelings. She was a passenger on this tiny seaplane that looked as if a strong wind might blow it out of the sky. Thanks to Tony Manzel, her editor at the *New York Tribune*, she was making her way to a remote Alaskan village in order to pursue a once-in-a-lifetime story. He'd made these travel plans without taking her fear of flying into consideration. He might as well have strapped her to the wing of the plane and shouted "Bon Voyage."

Two months ago, Tony had called her into his office and brought the story from a Juneau, Alaska, newspaper to her attention. Ever since then she hadn't been able to get it, or Mayor Jasper Prescott, out of her mind. The article, written by Jasper Prescott, had been sharp and savvy and moving. According to the mayor, the town of Love had experienced a mass exodus of female residents two decades ago. Since then they'd never been able to restore the male to female ratio in town. Add a cannery that had gone belly-up and dwindling income from local businesses, and it had all the markings of a recession.

"Finding Love in Alaska" had been the headline. It

had a certain ring to it. Jasper had thrown down the gauntlet and challenged single women to come to Love in pursuit of romance and fellowship. It was his belief that an influx of women would revitalize the town and bring back prosperity. He'd poured his heart out about his inability to prevent his own wife from leaving Love over thirty years ago due to the harsh climate, lack of sunlight and his own personal failings. She'd passed away of pneumonia in the Lower 48 before he could win her back. It was tragic and moving.

With stories like that, the town of Love was a gold mine.

If everything fell into place as she hoped it would, her time in Alaska would result in a major journalistic coup.

Dear Lord. Please don't let me die out here in the wilds of Alaska. I know You must think I'm pretty nervy asking You for favors since I haven't kept up with my faith, but I really could use Your help now. I'm out here on a wing and a prayer, Lord. Pun intended.

"Ladies, make sure you're buckled up," the pilot shouted. "We're about to make our final descent, and the wind is kicking up a bit."

Grace didn't like the sound of that. Wasn't there something really dangerous called wind shear? And maybe that clanking sound was the engine falling from the plane. She'd seen a news report about a plane making a crash landing after losing an engine. As a result of her terror, her body tensed up even more. She felt as if she might snap in two. In an unexpected act of bravery, she peeked out the window, gasping at the rate at which the ground was rising up to greet them. She could see massive trees and snow and churning water. Pressing her eyes closed, she began whispering unintelligible words. She clenched the armrest so tightly it felt as if her knuckles might break through her skin.

The plane lurched a bit to the right, causing her to let out a hoarse cry as it landed with a thud on the water. She leaned forward in her seat, placing her hands behind her head in crash position.

"We're here! We made it," Sophie announced in a peppy voice. "And so our adventure begins."

Slowly Grace opened her eyes. Sophie was smiling, her pretty face lit up with joy. Thankfully, they were still in one piece. Safe and sound. She let out a ragged breath. "On a wing and a prayer," she muttered. Her queasiness hadn't completely subsided, and the gentle rocking of the seaplane wasn't making things any better. If she'd eaten any lunch she would surely have lost it by now.

"Well, ladies, we've reached our final destination. Welcome to Love. It's been a pleasure flying with you. Thank you for flying O'Rourke Charters." The grinning golden-haired pilot, who looked as if he might moonlight as a model, stood up and ushered them toward the exit with a flourish of his hand. If she hadn't been so terrified about the flight, she might have noticed his chiseled features and broad shoulders. She vaguely remembered him introducing himself when she'd boarded the seaplane, but her mind had been consumed by the small size of the plane and her crippling fear of flying.

"Thank you for getting us here safely, Mr. O'Rourke," Sophie chirped as she grabbed her carry-on bag and stood up. "Come on, Grace. Alaska is waiting for us."

Love, Alaska, was a fishing village located fifty minutes from Anchorage, off the Pacific Ocean, on the southeastern tip of the state. Sparsely populated, there were fewer than a thousand residents. Once known for its wild

Alaskan salmon and halibut, Love's economy had fallen off in recent years, along with its abundant fish supply. For the next six weeks, this was home.

Grace zipped up her cranberry-colored down jacket and exited the seaplane on shaky legs. Her hand cradled her stomach as the waves of nausea continued to roll through her. She was blindly following Sophie, who was walking directly in front of her at a pretty fast clip. She heard Sophie cry out with a high-pitched squeal. Sophie stopped short, causing Grace to slam into the back of her. Grace found herself falling forward on the slippery pier with no way of catching herself. Suddenly she was being caught by a pair of strong, manly arms. She looked up, letting out a loud gasp as she laid eyes on the most ruggedly handsome man she'd ever seen in her life.

"Miss, are you all right?" His voice was low and husky yet smooth as silk at the same time. Wide-set, chocolate-brown eyes gazed into hers. Tiny flecks of gold ringed the pupils. Dark lashes framed his eyes. Sandy-brown hair peeked out from under his official-looking sheriff's hat. A cleft sat in the middle of his chin, serving, no doubt, as a stamp of approval on an indisputably gorgeous face.

She coughed to clear her throat, giving herself a few seconds to gain some composure. After all, she was a competent, professional journalist, not some moon-eyed schoolgirl. It wasn't as if he was the first nice-looking man she'd come across.

"F-fine. I'm fine," she said as he firmly set her down on the pier. She wobbled for a moment, taking a brief second to get her bearings. Once she collected herself she stood up while leaning heavily on his arm to support her weight. For the first time she noticed that her rescuer towered over her. Now that he'd straightened to his full height, she had to crane her neck to get a nice view of his face.

He scowled at her, his chiseled features only enhanced by his fierce expression. Being on the receiving end of his disapproval felt like being doused with a bucket of ice-cold water. Hmm. Maybe he wasn't as handsome as she'd first thought. He probably thought he was the cat's meow.

"Those shoes are an accident waiting to happen," he barked, his mouth set in grim lines. "This dock gets icy. You're going to break your neck wearing them."

Grace looked down at her midnight-black, designer heels. They'd cost her almost half of her weekly salary even though she'd bought them at a deep discount. Although she was grateful he'd saved her from falling on her face, she wasn't about to let him denigrate her shoes.

"These shoes are sheer perfection. I bought them at a sample sale. And the only reason I stumbled is because—" She shot a glance at Sophie, who was chatting up a storm with an older man with white hair and whiskers. A few school-aged children stood nearby holding brightly colored welcome signs. Sophie was way too sweet to hang out to dry. And perhaps it was the icy dock's fault after all. "It doesn't matter why I was such a klutz, but it has nothing to do with these shoes. I'm a pro at walking in heels."

"If you say so," he answered, his tone infused with doubt.

"Thanks for the save." She held out her hand. "Nice to meet you. I'm Grace. Grace Corbett."

"I'm Boone Prescott, town sheriff." His grip was firm as he shook her hand with an air of authority. Something about the way he carried himself convinced her that he was a no-nonsense kind of man. And if the lack of a wedding ring meant anything, he wasn't married. Not that it mattered any. She was here for a story and nothing else. Strictly business.

Her lips twitched at his introduction. Boone Prescott was the sheriff of Love. It sounded like a song. *I'm the sheriff of Love. Yeah, yeah, yeah.* Sheriff Prescott pointedly raised his eyebrow in her direction. His eyes narrowed, and he tilted his head to the side as he gazed at her. His expression was almost identical to the one her boss gave her when she'd said something outrageous. Oops! Had she actually just started humming and singing her "Sheriff of Love" song out loud? If she had to hazard a guess by the look on Boone's face, she had. And judging by his expression and the way he sauntered in the other direction, he was none too impressed by her vocal talents.

Boone stood at the end of the pier, his arms folded over his chest as he surveyed the mayhem swirling around him. It seemed as if every living, breathing male resident in town had decided to make an appearance today at the dock. He stroked his chin as he swept his gaze over the throng of people crowded around Grace and the other young woman with the fiery hair. He shook his head in disapproval at the men jockeying for position and jumping in to carry pieces of luggage for the two newcomers. They were acting like vultures.

Without meaning to, his eyes settled on Grace Corbett like laser beams. Unbidden, a sigh escaped his lips. Without a doubt, the woman was lovely. With her jet-black hair, blue eyes and creamy complexion, she had a unique, striking appearance. Her high-heeled shoes displayed her shapely legs to great advantage. She was bound to make a commotion in this small haven he called home. A slight tightening in his chest cavity accompanied that thought.

This time the sigh he let out was one of frustration. Why couldn't things be more simple? Why did his grandfather have to muddy the waters by advertising all over the United States about the sad state of affairs in Love? And why did Grace have to look so downright appealing, inappropriate shoes and all? Four-inch heels in the wilds of Alaska? He shook his head in disbelief. Grace was jaw-droppingly beautiful, but he wasn't about to give her a pass simply because she was the single most attractive woman who'd ever stepped foot into Love. For starters, she didn't seem to have a lick of good sense. Walking around in four-inch heels in an Alaskan fishing village was a recipe for disaster.

Didn't she know Alaska was a place filled with rugged terrain, unforgiving weather and a serious lack of fashion sense? On second thought, perhaps not. She looked every inch the city girl with her stylish down coat and fancy luggage. Her dark hair was adorned with a jeweled clip of some sort, and her makeup was flawless. He wasn't a big believer in eye shadow or lipstick, but on Grace it looked spectacular.

He chewed his lip. What in the world was this type of woman doing in Love? The question buzzed around him like an annoying gnat. She was as out of place as a polar bear on a tropical beach. He knew from past experience about city girls who tried to make it in Alaska. Been there, done that. He had the scars to prove it. Thinking about Diana didn't hurt half as much as it used to, he realized. Instead of feeling a stabbing pain in the region of his heart like he had in the past, all he felt now was regret.

He wished he hadn't spent all those weeks and months hurting over her. She really hadn't been worth his time.

"Enjoying the view, Sheriff?" Declan O'Rourke's familiar, teasing voice cut into his thoughts, serving as a much-needed reminder that he was still on the clock. Boone shot his best friend a look of annoyance and then made a point to look in another direction entirely. Now Grace Corbett was no longer in his line of sight. Although he could see a flash of cranberry in the corner of his eye, he willed himself not to look in her direction. It was easier said than done, he realized. Almost like not gazing at a glorious Alaskan full moon.

"No harm in looking, right?" Declan asked with a jab in his side.

He gritted his teeth. Maybe, just maybe, if he completely ignored Declan he would leave him alone.

"Did you see my two passengers? Can't remember the last time we had two beauty queens come to town." Declan let out a high-pitched whistle of appreciation. "Jasper really riled things up here, didn't he?"

At the mention of his grandfather, Boone raised an eyebrow. "Jasper doesn't know how not to shake things up. One of these days this experiment of his is going to blow up in his face."

Declan's mouth quirked. "It's not exactly an experiment, Boone. It was a call to action, a bid to save this town."

Boone let out a snort. "You sound just like him." He shook his head at the idea of his grandfather's crazy scheme being a good thing for the town. In the six short weeks of Operation Love, the town had been stirred up like a hornet's nest. Little by little, women had straggled into town. Twenty-two in all. Some had left on the next thing smoking, while others had lasted a little more than a week. So far, fourteen had stuck it out.

"Hey, the proof is in the pudding. Six couples already. Six!" Declan said in a triumphant voice.

"Doesn't matter if it's six or sixty. We'll see if they last," he answered with a sigh. "If they don't, there's going to be a lot of brokenhearted villagers. And even if this town has an abundance of women, it won't do anything to solve our fiscal problems. With the cannery gone, everyone's scrambling to come up with a way to bring income to town."

Silence hung in the air for a moment as they both absorbed the cold, harsh fact of the matter. True love was a beautiful thing, but it wasn't going to get the fishing cannery up and running, nor would it put money in the town's coffers. Although things weren't dire at the moment, a few years down the road it might all fall apart. Something needed to be done to turn things around, and he didn't think Operation Love was it.

Declan jerked his chin in the direction of the two women and the welcome wagon that had encircled them. "They're headed to the Moose. You going over? From the sounds of it, you could use a heavy dose of caffeine to pick up your mood."

The Moose Café, one of the town's most popular eating establishments, was owned by Boone's younger brother, Cameron. Situated in the center of town on Jarvis Street, directly across from the sheriff's office, it was a hangout for the locals. A few times a week Cameron brought in musicians who performed live for the customers. Other afternoons he allowed local artists to set up their painting and sculptures for sale. Although he himself wasn't a big coffee drinker, folks raved about all the varieties of coffee Cameron served up. From what he'd heard, he'd been branching out by offering lunch specials and baked goods. His brother had told him a few days ago that he was expecting new hires today, two women who were flying in to Anchorage from the Lower 48. Clearly, Grace was one of Cameron's new employees.

Somehow the image of Grace serving up java drinks, sourdough bread and cherry chocolate-chip cookies did not compute. He didn't know why, but the image struck him as off somehow. She seemed like the type of woman who dressed up to go work and always had a purse to match her outfit. He shook his head, wanting to free himself of any more thoughts of Grace. It wasn't as if he knew her, after all. He was merely speculating.

"No, thanks. I need to get back to the office." With a nod in Declan's direction, he turned on his heel and began walking back down the pier, right past Grace and her crowd of admirers. As he walked past, he couldn't help but look in her direction. She was staring right at him, a smile illuminating her face. She cheerily waved in his direction and called out to him. "See you later, Sheriff."

He raised his hand and waved back, stifling a mad urge to stick around and get to know Grace better. Something about the way she'd grinned at him warmed his insides. Even though he'd been testy with her earlier about her heels, she seemed willing to put her best foot forward. For the life of him he couldn't remember the last time he'd felt so conflicted about something. Or so intrigued. Even though his legs were carrying him in the opposite direction of Love's prettiest new resident, something inside him urged him to turn back around and stay a while.

As he settled himself behind the wheel of his cruiser, a dozen different questions were bouncing around his mind. Where had Grace come from in the Lower 48? Everything about her screamed city girl. Perhaps Boston, Chicago, Los Angeles or New York? Was it an adventurous spirit that had compelled her to relocate to Love? Or an open heart?

As images of Grace danced in his head, he couldn't help but remember that the last time he'd fallen for a city girl, his heart had been handed to him on a platter.

Welcome to Love. The prettied-up sign with the crooked letters hanging above the doorway of the Moose Café had made Grace want to shout with laughter. The establishment was as girly as a men's locker room. It was dark and dreary, all grays and browns, exuding an indisputably masculine vibe. Antlers hung on the wall, along with a dartboard and a retro framed print of a grizzly bear. Clearly, someone had wanted to impress the ladies by putting a few feminine touches in place. "Oh, this is lovely," Sophie had gushed. She'd raised her hands over her mouth, green eyes moist with emotion. "This is such a sweet gesture."

Sophie was right. It was thoughtful. And sweet. She wasn't used to either. As a journalist living in a metropolitan area, she operated in a high-pressure world. Competition among her peers for stories was fairly cutthroat. Although she got along well enough with her boss at the *Tribune*, Tony wasn't exactly the warm and fuzzy type. He'd never so much as given her a "thatta girl" or a thumbs-up. But that was all about to change, she thought. After she wrote this series on Love, Alaska, he'd be falling all over himself to pat her on the back. She might even get a promotion and a raise out of this, if she knocked it out of the park. Thoughts of a corner office with a view of Central Park danced in her head. She might even be eligible for a journalism award.

Within moments of entering the café the delicious aroma of baked goods wafted in the air. Grace lifted her nose in the air and sniffed. Cinnamon buns? Cookies? Whatever it was, the scent caused her stomach to grumble and her mouth to water. It had been hours since she'd eaten anything other than a stale bag of pretzels and a few handfuls of popcorn. She was famished.

"Ladies. Sophie and Grace, I presume." She saw Sophie's eyes widen as her jaw swung open. Grace followed her gaze until the trail stopped cold. The owner of the voice was tall and lean with chocolate-brown hair. Green-hazel eyes and a winning smile completed the picture.

What in the world was in the water supply in this town? No wonder women were giving up their lives in the 48 contiguous states and making tracks to Love. There were more hunky men in this fishing village than she'd seen in Manhattan in the past few weeks together. Operation Love should be renamed Operation Hotties.

"Hello. I'm Cameron Prescott, the owner. And your new boss." *Prescott?* As in related to the mind-bogglingly handsome Sheriff Boone Prescott? She studied him for a moment, recognizing the similarities between the two men. Although Cameron was Alaskan eye candy, the sight of him didn't pack the same sucker punch that his brother had. That was a good thing, since she was going to be working for Cameron at the Moose Café.

In all the hubbub, how could she have forgotten? She'd taken a job as a barista. As part of her cover story it had been important to find a paying job in town. It was also a great way to schmooze with the townsfolk and get a feel for Love. Since her skills were pretty much limited to writing for a living, her options had been slim to none. Tony had found this barista gig on an Alaskan job search website and sent in an application on her behalf. Lo and behold, she'd been hired. She stuck out her hand to Cameron, only to find herself being enveloped in a huge bear hug. Not knowing what else to do, she clung on for dear life. As soon as he let go of her, he reached for Sophie, giving her the same enthusiastic greeting. When he let go he stood back and rubbed his hands together. "I can't wait till tomorrow. This place should be pretty packed considering it's Cappuccino Tuesday—a free baked good with any cappuccino order. It's turning out to be a really great promotion. Hey," he said, his expression full of excitement. "Why don't I give you a quick tour of the kitchen? I promise to feed you afterward."

Grace groaned on the inside. This job was definitely going to be challenging, considering she'd only managed a two-week stint at Java Giant before she'd quit after realizing it was too stressful. Although the smell of coffee drifting through the air had been an incentive, she'd never gotten the hang of whipping up the drinks and serving the actual customers. She grimaced as memories of disgruntled, loud customers came into sharp focus. These coffee-holics took their drinks seriously, and they didn't take too kindly to inexperienced baristas messing up orders.

Fake it till you make it. That had always been her motto, and there was no need to switch things up at the moment. It had gotten her through some of the most difficult moments of her life. Gritting her teeth and smiling through the pain had served her well. There was no reason to switch things up now.

* * *

When the door to Boone's office crashed open without warning, his Alaskan malamute, Kona, emitted a low, menacing growl. The hairs stood up on the back of Kona's spine as the dog raced over to investigate.

"Hey, Kona. Good girl," Declan crooned as he nuzzled Kona's face and lavished her with the love and attention she craved. Within seconds Kona was wagging her tail and slobbering all over their visitor. Boone made a mental note to talk to his assistant, Shelly, about boundaries. Declan clearly had none, considering he never bothered to knock. His shameless flirting with Shelly gave Declan a direct line to his private office. All it took on his part was a wink and a smile.

Declan plunked himself down in one of the comfortable leather swivel chairs opposite Boone's desk. From past experience, Boone knew it was a sure sign he was planning to stay awhile.

Boone raised his head and subjected him to a fierce scowl. "I thought you were heading over to the Moose. From the sounds of it, the whole town is over there."

"I stopped in for an espresso," Declan said. "And a few of those churro treats Cameron makes."

Boone rolled his eyes at his best friend. A year ago he hadn't known an espresso from a hot chocolate. Now all of a sudden he was a connoisseur.

Declan leaned back in his chair and slowly began to stroke his chin. "So, I saw you talking to the dark-haired one earlier on the pier. Ginny. Georgia. I think that's her name."

"Grace," he said, his tone clipped. "Grace Corbett."

Declan shot him a knowing look textured with twenty-plus years of friendship. "So, you got your eye on her, huh?"

Boone leveled a category-five glare at his best friend. "No, I do not have my eye on Grace Corbett. Despite my grandfather's grand scheme to bring marriageable women and marry off the single men in town, I want nothing to do with it. And if I did want to fall in love and settle down, I certainly wouldn't hand-select a woman who doesn't have the brains God gave a goose." Settling back in his chair, Boone let loose with a loud harrumph. "Sky-high heels. It's a wonder she didn't break her neck."

Declan swung his feet onto the edge of Boone's desk and leaned back in his chair, his hands propped behind his head. A wide grin showcased a set of pearly whites. "Well, it's a good thing you're not interested, 'cause there are a few men already staking their claim."

Boone shot up in his chair. "Staking a claim? They aren't pieces of property to be claimed, Declan. It's chauvinistic comments like yours that got us into this sad situation in the first place."

Declan waved a hand in the air. "Take it easy. I didn't mean it like that. And I'm not taking responsibility for the woman shortage in this town. Those ripples started when we were barely a twinkle in our parents' eyes."

Boone lowered his head and tried to focus on the report set out before him on his desk. "So, who's circling around Grace?" His voice came out gruffer than he'd intended.

"Why don't you come with me to the Moose Café and find out for yourself?" Declan tossed out the invitation with all the grace of a major-league pitcher. He stood up from his chair, a sly grin etched on his face.

Humph, he thought grumpily. It was classic Declan to dangle a carrot in front of his nose, knowing he could never resist a challenge being thrown down. He'd been doing it ever since they were in the second grade. With a loud groan he surrendered, pushing himself away from his desk and making his way toward his office door. Much to his chagrin, his curiosity had gotten the better of him. Kona cocked her head to the side and proceeded to trail after him. With a quick hand signal and a one-word command, he had Kona settled back down in her dog bed.

With his best friend following behind him, Boone wrenched his office door open and strode down the hall past his bewildered-looking receptionist.

"I thought you were in for the rest of the afternoon," Shelly called out after him.

"I thought so, too," he mumbled as he strode out the door and beat a fast path across the street to the Moose Café.

Cameron beamed with pride as he finished the grand tour and led them back into the main dining area of the café. While they were in the kitchen, Sophie had asked all the right questions—while Grace had been praying that Cameron wouldn't ask too many questions about their previous work experience as baristas. It was nice to see that Cameron was so gung ho about the Moose Café and all its trimmings. "It sure is beautiful," Sophie said, her tone brimming with enthusiasm.

"Thanks. It's my pride and joy. Why don't the two of you take a seat and I'll bring you something to eat?" He gestured toward the dining area. The crowd literally parted as they made their way to one of the tables by the window. There were lots of curious stares and hats tipped in their direction. Several men rushed forward to pull their chairs out for them and stick menus in their hands. Sophie was all polite smiles and thank-yous while Grace was still trying to figure out how she was going to wing it as a barista. Thankfully the place was only open six hours a day.

When she went to sit down she found the chair in front of her being wrenched to the left and then to the right. And back again. Two men were having a tug-of-war over the chair. They'd introduced themselves to her and Sophie earlier at the dock, although for the life of her she couldn't remember either of their names. Henry? Theodore? She held up her hands, prepared to tell both of them to knock it off when they released the chair and began poking each other in the chest.

The sound of a sharp whistle rent the air. "Hey! What's going on here?" She blinked in surprise to see Sheriff Boone at her side, his arm encircling her back in a protective gesture. He gently pushed her aside before stepping in between the two adversaries. He looked at one, then the other, his expression forbidding. "I hope neither one of you is doing anything that might warrant a trip to the sheriff's office." He continued to swing his gaze back and forth between both men. "I think it's best to shake hands and apologize to the ladies for being overzealous."

The two men hung their heads, grudgingly shook hands and then mumbled brief words of apology before stepping into the background. Grace almost felt sorry for them. They'd slunk off like polecats.

What in the world had just happened? Had two men actually been fighting over her in an Alaskan coffeehouse?

Boone looked down at his watch and then pointedly back to her. "Congratulations, Miss Corbett. You've been in town for less than an hour, and you already have grown men fighting over you."

Chapter Two

Heat warmed her cheeks as a result of Sheriff Prescott's comment. Was she really being blamed for the mayhem that had just erupted? The last thing she wanted was for two local yokels to duke it out for her time and attention. She made a mental note to add this to her column for the *Tribune*. Men shamelessly brawling over a single woman in a local eating establishment. The sheriff of Love forced to break things up. It was thrilling to see how quickly anecdotes for her articles were beginning to materialize. Yet it was annoying to be blamed for something she'd had no part in.

"I never wanted… I didn't mean to—" she stammered, instantly losing her composure under the heat of his gaze.

His grin was slow in the making, but bit by bit it broke over his face until it seemed as if it stretched from ear to ear. Brown eyes twinkled. Little crinkles gathered near his eyes. "I'm teasing you. Seth and Thomas fight over every little thing under the sun. If they weren't fighting over you, it would have been over who was picking up the tab or which one of 'em caught the biggest fish."

Relief swept through her. For some reason she didn't

want the sheriff to think she was starting trouble on her first day in Love. She smiled back at him, feeling a bit dazzled by his pearly whites and effortless charm. He pulled back her chair and gestured for her to sit down. From her seat across from Grace, Sophie was beaming at Sheriff Prescott as if he'd just achieved world peace. Before she could make the introductions, Sophie stuck out her hand. "Howdy. I'm Sophie Miller. Nice to meet the man who keeps law and order in this town."

"Sheriff Boone Prescott," he said, reaching out to shake Sophie's hand. "I do my best to keep this town orderly."

Prescott? Prescott? The name was now ringing in her ears. She'd heard that name before ever stepping foot into town. What was it about that name? It was on the tip of her tongue. *Ahh, yes!*

It was Mayor Jasper Prescott who had written the original article about Love, inviting single women to come to his hometown to find romance and to help solve the woman shortage. It was because of Jasper that she'd come up with the idea to write the column about this town and its residents. Now that she was here, she didn't know whether to thank him or kick him in the shins.

"Hey," she said, looking up at Boone. "Are you any relation to Jasper Prescott, the town mayor?"

"He sure is." A raspy voice sounded over her shoulder. She turned her head to see a white haired, whiskered man beaming at her as if he'd been lit up from the inside with a lightbulb. "I'm his grandfather." He swung his gaze back and forth between her and Sophie, his expression full of joy. "It's nice to see that Operation Love is in full effect." He reached over and clapped his grandson on the shoulder. "So, which one of you two lovely ladies is going to take Boone off the market and make me a great-grandfather again?"

Boone cringed at his grandfather's none-too-subtle attempt to get him married off. He shouldn't be surprised, considering this wasn't the first time he'd tried to play matchmaker on his behalf. Normally, he had the good manners not to mention great-grandchildren. His brother Liam had already given Jasper those bragging rights when his son Aidan was born. At the moment it didn't seem to matter to Jasper. This time he was clearly going for broke. In response to his pronouncement, Grace's blue eyes began to blink like a startled owl while Sophie giggled with delight.

"Settle down now, Jasper," Boone said, trying to shrug off the waves of embarrassment. He didn't know why Jasper's meddling was getting to him, since he usually just shook his head and laughed it off. Perhaps it was because of a certain raven-haired newcomer who'd piqued his interest the moment she'd stumbled into his arms. It had been a long time since he'd cared what a woman thought about him, but strangely enough, it mattered to him in this very moment. He didn't know why, but Grace Corbett's opinion mattered.

"Hot food coming through." The loud announcement preceded Cameron's appearance at the table. He was carrying a large tray filled with drinks and a wide assortment of food. Was it his imagination or was Cameron now serving a much wider variety of foods than he'd realized? He didn't remember sandwiches being on the menu, or little pizzas. "Hey, Boone." Cameron acknowledged him with a nod as he deposited plates brimming with food in front of Sophie and Grace. He placed a steaming mug next to each of their plates. "I thought you'd given up coffee."

"I didn't stop drinking coffee, Cam," he explained for what felt like the tenth time. "I'm just not a big fan of those frothy, foamy drinks you specialize in. They're all tongue twisters, too. A half cup of mocha latte or an iced caramel macchiato with a twist of cinnamon. I like to know what I'm drinking."

"Don't knock 'em. Those specialty drinks have put this place on the map," Cameron answered, a slight edge to his voice.

Boone chuckled. There was a running joke in his family about the Moose Café saving the town from financial ruin. Although the place was doing well, it was a far cry from being Love's salvation. Perhaps he didn't say it very often, but he was proud of the way Cameron had turned his life around and made a full-fledged success of his café. If only they could get back to the way things had been between them before everything had fallen apart right along with the cannery deal.

When Cameron had been swindled by his girlfriend's father and subsequently lost a great sum of the town's money, it had been hard to find anyone in town to take up for him. He'd been the town's whipping boy. Boone had tried to defend his brother, but the more he uncovered about the stolen money, the angrier he'd become at Cameron. He'd been so in love with Paige that he'd made foolish, reckless mistakes. And because of it, the whole town of Love had suffered the financial consequences. They'd exchanged words one evening, taking nasty jabs at each other, which were hard to repair in the light of day. Ever since then things had been shaky between them.

Boone watched as Grace picked up her sandwich with

both hands and took a big bite out of it. She let out a sigh of appreciation. "This is delicious," she raved, placing her hand over her mouth as she spoke. She swallowed and took another bite.

"What is it?" Sophie asked, taking a daintier bite of her sandwich. "It's yummy."

"Smoked turkey breast with fresh avocado, some crispy bacon and a blue-cheese spread. I'm expanding the menu to attract more culinary-minded customers."

Jasper waved his hand in the air and plunked himself down in one of the empty chairs. He propped his elbows on the table and said, "Enough about the menu. I want to know what Sophie and Grace think about our little village."

"They've only been here for an hour," Boone said, shooting his grandfather a warning look. "Let them settle in before you subject them to the grand inquisition."

Cameron shook his head and threw his hands in the air. "I've got to take some orders. Hazel must be swamped in the kitchen."

Hazel Tookes, owner of the Black Bear Cabins, was a beloved figure in town. In her late sixties, she was an honorary auntie to the Prescott brothers. With her silver hair and piercing green eyes, she was a striking figure. Over the years she'd picked up a lot of the slack in his parents' absence. Hazel came in a few times a week to help out Cameron in the kitchen and to waitress.

Sophie jumped up from her chair, an eager expression stamped on her face. She bit her lip. "I'd like to make myself useful behind the counter. I'm pretty good at making drinks."

Cameron shoved his hand through his hair and looked

around at the crowd. "That would be great. With all these people in here, I can use all the help I can get."

Boone's brother sent him a commiserating look as he walked away with Sophie. They both knew the drill. Jasper was about to start pontificating about the benefits of living in Love, Alaska.

"Forgive me. I'm getting ahead of myself." Jasper reached for Grace's hand and raised it to his lips, placing a gentle kiss on it. "I met Miss Miller earlier on the pier, so I'm assuming you must be Grace Corbett from New York. It's a pleasure to make your acquaintance. I'd be happy if you called me Jasper."

So his hunch about Grace had been correct. She was a city girl, hailing all the way from the Big Apple. Boone deposited himself in the chair vacated by Sophie. He didn't dare leave his grandfather alone with Grace. There was no telling what nonsense might come out of his mouth that might send her on the first seaplane back to Anchorage. The very thought of her leaving caused a trickle of discomfort to flow through him.

Jasper continued. "Welcome to Love, my dear. May your journey be one of discovery."

Grace crinkled her nose. "Discovery?"

"Isn't that what brought you here?" Jasper asked. "A need to find out more about yourself and the world around you?"

Grace shrugged. "In your article you said there was a need for women here in Love. That's why I'm here. Not sure about the discovery part."

Jasper chuckled, a low rumble emanating from his chest. "Don't worry, Grace. I'm seventy-five years old, but I'm still on the trail of several discoveries. Town legend says that a wise leader will find rivers of gold. I'm aiming to be that leader."

"Legend? What legend?" Grace leaned forward in her seat, her blue eyes dancing with excitement. There was such a sweet look of rapture etched on Grace's face. For a moment she resembled a small child who'd been promised the sun, sky and moon.

A slow hiss escaped Boone's lips. "Don't get him started," he warned in a low voice. He shook his head at Jasper. "You're treading on thin ice."

Jasper leaned in toward Grace, his voice lowering to a stage whisper. "There's treasure hidden in Love, buried here by one of our ancestors after the Gold Rush. I'm determined to find it. Not for selfish gain, but for the betterment of this town and our community."

Boone could still hear every word his grandfather uttered, even though Jasper was doing his best to whisper. Although it wasn't anything he hadn't heard before, he felt as if he was absorbing it anew through Grace's perspective. She could be thinking he was a lovable curmudgeon or a raving lunatic. It could go either way.

Grace's mouth now hung open. Boone couldn't tell whether she was incredulous or impressed by Jasper's fanciful tale of gold, hidden treasure and his determination to find it.

"You have a standing invitation to come by my office any time you like and get a personal tour of Love." He winked at her. "And I might just let you come treasure hunting with me."

Grace wagged her finger at him. "You better not be teasing me. It sounds like a wonderful adventure. I'm looking forward to it."

Jasper slowly got to his feet and nodded his head in

Grace's direction. "I have to get back to my office and sign a few ordinances. It has truly been a pleasure to make your acquaintance."

Watching his grandfather shuffle away filled Boone's heart with a mixture of pride and sadness. Jasper wasn't getting any younger, and his physical decline in recent years had been noticeable. Despite suffering a heart attack a year ago and dealing with chronic arthritis, Jasper still continued to proudly serve as mayor. He'd been serving in that capacity for nearly two decades. Even though Boone thought "Operation Love" was an over-the-top, desperate tactic, he admired Jasper's passion and the way he'd put himself out there for the world to see, warts and all. Sometimes he worried about his own inability to step out on the ledge and take a risk. For so long now, everything in his life had been nice and comfortable. What was it his father used to say? "No risk, no reward."

Silence settled over the table in the wake of Jasper's departure. What now? Idle chitchat? Meaningless conversation? *How about this bone-chilling Alaska weather we're having? Do you come to coffee bars often?* He was so out of practice making conversation with an attractive woman, it was downright pitiful. Perhaps he could use a few pointers from his grandfather, who hadn't skipped a beat in his discussion with Grace.

Boone made the mistake of glancing around the café as his mind raced with things to say to Grace. A few men in town were openly glaring at him, clearly upset that he was spending time with one of the new arrivals in town. Ha! Some of them had no business even trying to talk to Grace. Hugo had been married and divorced three times over while Dean scared off most women once they realized he reeked of his bison farm. Ricky Stanton was staring at Grace with a forlorn expression etched on his face, a clump of droopy flowers clutched in his hand. Deciding to flex his muscles a little bit, Boone edged a little closer to Grace. Declan gave him a thumbs-up sign from his seat at the counter.

"I really admire Jasper's gusto," Grace said. "He seems like the sort of person who lives his life with conviction." There was a wistful tone in her voice that made him curious about who Grace Corbett was as a person. Was she living life to the fullest? Or just existing? Had her heart led her all the way to Love? Or was she looking to shake things up in her world?

"You're right about Jasper. He lives life to the fullest in a no-holds-barred kind of way. He's had a few health scares recently, so I wish he would settle down some, but he's pretty ornery. Please don't take his comments about the legend to heart. This town is his whole life, and he'd believe in almost anything that might help us out of this financial setback. Hope is a wonderful thing, but banking on centuries-old treasure is kind of pie in the sky."

Grace jutted out her chin. "I think it's wonderful that he believes in something, especially after all he's been through."

Boone frowned. "So you read the article? And what he said about losing my grandmother?"

She nodded, her eyes radiating compassion. "Yes, I did. It was one of the most moving things I've ever read. Loving someone and losing them is a terrible thing."

Boone shuddered as a dozen different thoughts roared through him. On the one hand, it didn't sit well with him that Jasper had aired the family's dirty laundry for all to see and read about with their morning coffee and Danish. On the other hand, it had been Jasper's story to tell. He'd lived it. And Boone had no right to judge him for it. He'd done it for the greater good—to inspire women to move lock, stock and barrel to the place his family called home.

"He laid himself bare in that article, all in the hopes of inspiring women to come to Love and plant roots here. But Operation Love might not work out the way he's envisioned. I don't want him to get his heart broken all over again." There was a ragged little catch to his voice, one born of suppressed emotion and tenderness. He locked eyes with Grace, and he knew she'd heard the emotion in his voice. He could see it reflected back at him in her eyes.

Grace's expression fell, and she appeared shaken by his comment. "I'm not sure you can protect him against a broken heart, no matter how badly you might want to. Take it from me, hearts don't come with a warning label."

By late afternoon, the crowd at the Moose Café had dwindled to a few stragglers. Sheriff Prescott had taken off shortly after she made her comment about broken hearts. Judging by his reaction, it fell under the category of "too much information." She shouldn't be surprised. Most men shied away from conversations about feelings and heartache. Come to think of it, so did she. But there had been something so poignant and genuine about his desire to protect his grandfather. It had cracked her wide open.

Hearts don't come with a warning label. Ugh! She couldn't believe those words had tumbled off her lips. There must be something in the Alaskan air that caused blabber-itis. She wouldn't make that mistake again.

After Cameron shut down the kitchen and coffee bar he laid out some basic rules about working for him. He seemed like a pretty laid-back and reasonable boss. He gave each of them a uniform—a custom designed T-shirt with a big brown moose on it. The words, *Got coffee?* had been printed on one of the antlers. There were also a pair of sweatpants with the words *Moose Café* printed down the side of one leg. Grace didn't know what was more upsetting. The ugly brown uniform or the idea of coming to work tomorrow as a barista. She chewed on her lip, wondering if she should pull Cameron aside and confess her lack of real-world experience as a barista.

No, she couldn't do it. It might cast her in a bad light and draw suspicion on her. She didn't need anyone in Love questioning her reasons for being in Alaska. This series would rise and fall on the real-life experiences of the townsfolk. If she couldn't get them to trust her and talk freely with her about their trials and tribulations, as well as the woman shortage…there would be no series. If they had any reason to suspect her, they might clam up. She was just going to have to channel her inner barista and do her best to whip up the best coffee drinks ever served at the Moose Café.

Since she and Sophie were both going to be living at the Black Bear Cabins, Hazel, their new landlord, had offered to drive them over. Grace was feeling a little jet-lagged after the long flight and the meet and greet with the residents of Love. It would be nice to get into some comfy clothes and relax. Something about the dark, dreary climate was making her more tired than usual. Not to mention that her fingers were itching to write up some of her observations on her computer before she settled in for the night.

The moment they stepped outside she noticed the sign reading Sheriff's Department tacked on to the building directly across the street. She let out a sigh. Having the easy-on-the-eyes sheriff so close by might not be such a good thing. Being in Love had nothing to do with discovery or making a match with a hunky Alaskan man. It was all about her job. Staying here in Alaska for six weeks was a means to an end. This series about the citizens of Love, Alaska, would sell itself. All she had to do was write meaty articles and sprinkle them with slices of everyday life in this charming hamlet.

The minute Jasper had started talking about the Gold Rush and lost treasure, he'd totally captured her attention. It was the perfect angle for the piece. It added a historical perspective and a folksy charm that would hook readers. She brushed aside the kernel of guilt gnawing at her. There was no doubt in her mind that she would be subjecting this small village to considerable media once her piece about buried treasure in Love hit the presses. She prayed it wouldn't turn into a media circus with treasure hunters descending on the fishing village in pursuit of riches.

It's not my problem, she reminded herself. Eyes on the prize. In six weeks' time this town would be nothing more than a memory for her. The only person she had any allegiance to was herself. And her job at the *New York Tribune*.

"It's only about an eight-minute drive to the cabins," Hazel explained as she navigated her truck along the snow-covered streets of downtown Love. Grace quietly took in all the quaint shops along Jarvis Street as Sophie chattered away in the front seat. There was a barbershop, a small bookstore called The Bookworm, a trading post, a post office and a pawnshop. Grace wrinkled her nose. Where were the nail salon and the beauty shop? Had her research led her astray? She'd been certain that at least one beauty shop existed in Love. Perhaps it had closed down or it wasn't located in the center of town. Maybe nails and hair weren't deemed important here.

"How do you drive in all this snow?" Grace asked, her eyes transfixed by the snowflakes swirling through the air. It fascinated her to see Hazel tackling the rugged, icy terrain as if it was no big deal.

"As long as I have my all-wheel drive and studded tires, I'm good. You get used to driving in snow and ice in this type of climate. We're heading into the rainy season, too, which has its own challenges. Luckily, winters aren't as brutal here on the coast as they are in the interior. At least here in Love we can enjoy outdoor activities without freezing our tails off."

Nope! Grace thought. Freezing her tail off was definitely not an option.

Along the way they passed a few other cars and some townsfolk. Each and every time, Hazel tooted her horn and waved. If nothing else, Grace got the impression that the folks here in town were part of a tight-knit community. In New York, people typically honked their horns as a sign of annoyance and rarely as a way of greeting their neighbors.

They sped by several moose-crossing signs, a sight that caused Grace to take out her camera and snap a few pictures. Although she had no idea what happened when you ran across a moose, the very idea of it seemed surreal. When Hazel turned off the main road, a faded, rusted sign announced the Black Bear Cabins. Snow-covered trees lined the lane leading to the property. Beautiful white-capped mountains loomed in the distance, serving as a reminder that she was in a completely different world than the one she normally inhabited. The cabins were a reddish brown color and were rustic in appearance. Each one had a porch out front with two Adirondack chairs filling up the small space.

Hazel helped them lug their suitcases to their front porches. As she made her way to her new lodging, snow and ice seeped into her shoes, bringing into sharp focus her earlier conversation with the sheriff of Love. She hated to admit it, but her shoe choice hadn't been practical. Sooner rather than later, she was going to have to dig out her furry, heeled boots.

Their new landlord took out a key and opened up the cabin door. She ushered them in with a flourish, extending her hand as she said, "Here are your digs. Living room, kitchen, bed and bath. Nothing fancy, but it's warm and safe." She handed Sophie another key. "Your place is next door. If you need anything I'm at the lodge right down the road. There's a blue rock outside poking through the snow. You can't miss it." Before Grace could blink, Hazel was gone.

Grace frowned as she looked around the utilitarian cabin. Every single thing in the cabin was brown and no-frills. She had a sudden flashback to Camp Hiawatha, the overnight camp her parents had stuck her for three long weeks when she'd been twelve. The word *bleak* instantly came to mind. "This place is—"

"Full of possibilities," Sophie interjected.

Grace turned toward the closest thing she had to a friend in Love. Although she was hoping to see a look of dismay on her face, all she saw was a perky little smile. She dropped her bags to the hardwood floor with a thud and heaved a tremendous sigh. She liked Sophie an awful lot, but there was no way on Earth she could fix this situation. As far as Grace was concerned, the next six weeks couldn't go by fast enough.

Chapter Three

Boone put his feet up on his desk and settled back in his chair, his hands braced behind his head as he made himself comfortable. Although his shift was officially done, he planned on hanging out at his office for a bit longer.

It wasn't as if he had anything to go home to at night. Maybe if Kona was a stay-at-home dog, Boone would be raring to leave the office after a full day's work, if only to reunite with his four-legged friend. So far, being at the sheriff's office trumped going home to an empty house. With every passing day he was beginning to realize that God hadn't intended him to walk through life alone. Lately, there had been a relentless ache inside him. A desire to settle down. An unwillingness to spend another Valentine's Day without a special someone in his life. Perhaps Operation Love wasn't such a crazy idea after all.

He shook his head and chuckled at the memory of Thomas and Seth fighting over Grace. Although he didn't advocate using one's fists to solve problems, he had to admit that a woman like Grace Corbett might cause a man to get carried away. One look into those sapphire-blue eyes and a person could start thinking of things he'd avoided for a long time.

He was so wrapped up in his thoughts, he barely heard the rapping on his office door. Shelly peered in, orange curls bouncing as she bobbed her head. "I just fielded a call from one of the ladies staying at the Black Bear Cabins. She identified herself as Grace Corbett."

Grace? Shelly now had his undivided attention. He swung his legs off the desk and sat up ramrod straight in his chair. "What's the problem?"

"She said she's trapped inside her cabin with a wild animal."

Grace sat on the front porch of her cabin, her arms wrapped around her middle as the cold night air began to whip relentlessly against her body. It was fair to say that Sophie must sleep like the dead since she hadn't emerged from her cabin despite Grace's desperate cries for help. Nor had she answered her door when Grace had banged on it a few minutes ago. Her current predicament was courtesy of one onyx-colored animal who'd scampered across the living room and scooted under the sofa. For more terrifying minutes than she wanted to admit, she'd stayed frozen in place, afraid to move an inch lest her movement provoked the creature to come out of hiding and attack her.

She'd cried out for help to no avail. She didn't even have Hazel's phone number. Feeling desperate, she'd reached for her cell phone and dialed 911 to report the emergency situation. Once she'd gathered her courage to make a break for it, she'd dashed to the front door and escaped. In her panic she'd forgotten to grab her coat. Oh, well. She'd rather freeze to death than venture back into the cabin and run the risk of coming face-to-face with the creature. In the brief seconds she'd laid eyes on him, he'd seemed vicious and mean. She'd seen fangs. Of that she was certain.

Within the space of five minutes she heard the sound of tires crunching against the snow and ice in the driveway. A blue-and-white cruiser quickly came into view, illuminated by the glowing porch light. Once the car pulled up in front of the cabin, she watched as none other than Sheriff Boone Prescott emerged from the cruiser. She'd recognize those broad shoulders of his anywhere. In all her life she didn't think she'd ever been happier to see anyone. In the face of this crisis, he seemed even bigger and broader and manlier than he'd appeared to be earlier this afternoon.

He tipped his sheriff's hat at her. "Third time I've seen you today, Miss Corbett. I'm getting a strong suspicion you missed me."

Annoyance flooded her. "Can you please stop calling me Miss Corbett? My name is Grace. You make me sound like someone's spinster aunt. And might I add that your ego is in rare form, Sheriff Prescott. I called your office because of the creature in my cabin, not in order to see you again."

He chuckled, seemingly amused by her mild outrage. "If I'm to call you Grace, you're going to have to call me Boone."

She nodded. *Boone.* The name fit him. It was manly and rugged and strong. Just like the sheriff himself. "Okay. Boone it is. Although I'd love to exchange more pleasantries, there's a creature inside," she said curtly. "And it's getting mighty cold out here." She wrapped her arms around her middle, her teeth beginning to chatter.

Why hadn't she grabbed her coat? Oh, yeah. She'd been afraid of being eaten alive.

He knit his brows together. "A creature? Can you be more specific?"

Grace shivered. It was freezing out here, and the thought of the critter inside her cabin was making her feel a little crazy. What if it was rummaging through all her things and tearing up her clothes? Or ripping apart her favorite pair of shoes?

The sheriff shrugged off his jacket and draped it around her back and shoulders. "Thank you," she murmured as a woodsy scent assailed her senses.

"The creature," he prodded, his eyes dark and probing.

"It was big and black…and it hissed at me. I saw teeth…huge, white teeth. Fangs, I believe. And I saw a flash of white, so it may have been foaming at the mouth."

"A big, black, hissing, foaming-at-the-mouth creature?" Boone flung the question at her in a skeptical manner. His perfectly shaped lips twitched.

She put her hands on her hips and made a huffing sound. "Yes. That's exactly right. I know what I saw. It's engrained in my mind."

"Why don't you go sit in my cruiser where it's warm while I check things out? Wouldn't want you to freeze to death on your first night in town."

She didn't want to be safely ensconced in Boone's cruiser while a story was unfolding mere feet away from her. As a journalist, it simply wasn't her way. She wanted to be where the action was taking place, in the event she needed to write about it later. Plus, she had every faith in Boone's ability to keep her safe from being mauled or attacked. Faith. It was funny to feel the first stirrings of faith after going so long without it. "I'll stay right behind you, if that's okay," she said.

The sheriff's eyes widened almost imperceptibly, but he nodded and walked toward her cabin door. He wrenched the door open and strode inside, flipping the light on as he entered.

"Where did you last see it?" he asked in a low voice. His eyes were darting all over the room, his body primed for action.

She pointed a shaking finger in the direction of the russet couch. "There. It went under there." She moved backward a few steps until she was standing next to the open door. If things went south at least she would have an escape hatch.

Boone went over to the couch and rattled it with both hands. Despite the shaking, nothing emerged. He got down on his knees and peered under the sofa. The side of his face was pressed against the hardwood floors.

"Be careful!" she cried out. She'd watched enough episodes of *When Animals Attack* to know that this could end badly.

Dear Lord, please don't let any harm come to the sheriff. Or to me. I'm trying to be brave about this Alaska experience, but it's hard to be strong when there's a wild animal on the loose in my cabin. And even though Boone was snarky about my shoes this morning, he seems like a good person.

Boone scrambled to his feet and lifted the couch up off the ground, swiveling it as he dropped it down a few feet away. Grace let out a scream as the creature emerged and scooted toward Boone. She watched in horror as he bent down and scooped it up in his arms.

Oddly enough, he seemed as placid as a lake in summer. He hadn't even flinched.

He sent her a pearly grin. Butterflies fluttered low in her stomach. She wasn't sure if it was due to Boone's charm or the unexpected drama unfolding before her eyes. "Grace, meet Primrose. Primrose, this is Grace. She came all the way from New York City, so you can't camp out in her cabin and scare the daylights out of her."

"Is that a…skunk?" she asked, noticing for the first time the white stripe trailing down the creature's back.

"Sure is. She belongs to Hazel. She's been de-scented, so there's no risk of being sprayed by her."

"This is someone's pet?" Her voice came out squeaky and high-pitched. Boone was patting Primrose on the head and nuzzling her under her chin.

Boone rocked back on the heels of his boots. He appeared to be fighting back a smirk. "Not a pet, exactly, since skunk ownership isn't legal in Alaska. Hazel has an exhibitor's license for her. She takes Primrose to schools, wildlife symposiums, fairs and such. She must have gotten loose."

She craned her neck to get a better look. "She doesn't bite?"

"She's domesticated. Hazel raised her from a newborn. Skunks aren't indigenous to Alaska, but Hazel's put a lot of love and care into her. She actually rescued her from certain death."

Grace took a few steps forward until she was standing next to Boone and Primrose. She reached out and tentatively patted her on her back. Truth to be told, Primrose was pretty cute for a skunk.

"See? There's nothing to fear but fear itself." Boone looked down at her and their gazes locked for a moment.

They were standing mere inches from one another with only Primrose separating them. Something was brewing in the air, some hint of awareness that hummed and pulsed in the atmosphere.

"There you are, Primrose. I've been looking all over the place for you." Hazel's voice rang out in the silence, shattering the moment before Grace could even put her finger on what had happened between her and the sheriff.

Boone placed Primrose in Hazel's arms, his movements full of tenderness. "She gave Grace a bit of a scare. It's not every day a skunk shows up in one's home."

Hearing Boone refer to the cabin as her home was jarring. This bare-bones cabin was a far cry from her cozy apartment in Soho, which she'd purchased with her inheritance from her grandfather. Perhaps if the cabin wasn't so drab, she would feel a little more comfortable living here.

"She's really quite harmless. Just a nuisance is all," Hazel explained in an apologetic tone. She nestled her face in Primrose's fur as she cradled her like a baby. "Thanks for finding her, Grace. I owe you one. You too, Boone." With a wave of her hand, Hazel was gone, swallowed up by the onyx night as she made her way back to her lodgings.

"Sorry for the commotion," Grace said sheepishly. She bit her lip and looked down at the floor. She felt like the world's biggest fool. She hadn't even been in Love a full day before she'd had to make an emergency phone call to law enforcement. And her big bad creature had ended up being a domesticated skunk. She hadn't even been in danger of being sprayed by noxious fumes.

"No problem. It's been a while since I had to rescue someone from a wild, dangerous, foaming-at-the-mouth creature." Once again she found herself on the receiving end of a beautiful smile.

Unable to stop herself, she let out a whoop of laughter. Now that Boone put it that way, it was rib-tickling hilarious. All the stress and tension faded away. It felt good to laugh out loud at something. She couldn't remember the last time she'd done so. It was hard to wrap her head around how lonely and mirthless her life in New York had become over the past few years. Always being on the move had distracted her from this simple fact.

She'd been so afraid while she'd been alone in the cabin, yet the moment Boone had shown up, those fears had dissipated. Staying in the cabin while he hunted down the creature had been an act of bravery. For a woman who'd lost her faith a long time ago, today had been full of surprises. She'd flown all the way to Alaska, and in the process, confronted her fear of flying head-on. And tomorrow she was beginning her new job as a barista, even though she didn't have a clue how to make specialty coffee drinks. All in all, she was operating way out of her comfort zone.

Boone folded his arms across his chest, striking a commanding pose. "Was this the closest you've ever been to wildlife?"

Grace nodded. "Other than the Bronx Zoo, yes. My family didn't even own a pet when I was growing up."

He shook his head, his expression radiating disbelief. "Not a single one? Not even a fish or a hamster?" When Grace shook her head again, he continued. "We had so many pets our house resembled a menagerie." Their laughter mingled together as one, creating a beautiful harmony.

"So, you really came all the way here because of Jasper's article?" His smile was nice and easy. The little dimple in his chin stood out even more when he grinned.

"Yes, I did," she answered. "It really spoke to me." A feeling of relief swept through her. It wasn't a lie at all. Just a little bending of the truth. It was definitely because of Jasper Prescott that she'd ended up in Love, Alaska. Only not for the reason Boone believed. Not in pursuit of love.

He let out a soft whistle. "Well then, the single men of Love owe Jasper a debt of gratitude."

"Why's that?" she asked, curiosity overtaking her.

"Because you, Grace Corbett, are the most stunning woman this town has ever seen."

The compliment took Grace by surprise. It washed over her like a gentle summer rain after a scorching heat wave. When she'd asked the question she hadn't been angling for praise. It wasn't something she received often, so to have Boone pay her such a kindness warmed her insides. Her cheeks felt warm and she self-consciously tucked her chin into her chest. It was an odd little habit she had when she was nervous. A protective gesture of sorts.

Boone reached out and gently touched her chin, lifting it up so that their eyes met. "I didn't mean to embarrass you. Just speaking a plain truth."

"Thank you. Not just for the compliment, but for coming out here to assist me. Now I can close my eyes tonight without having to worry."

He shifted from one foot to another. "I should be getting back to town," Boone said as he gestured toward the door. "You must be tuckered out."

Grace trailed behind Boone as he ambled outside.

Once he reached the porch, he turned toward her, his expression difficult to read.

She looked past him, distracted by the brilliant stars peeking out through a midnight sky. She let out a surprised cry. "Oh, it's stunning," she gasped. Boone turned his head and looked up. In profile his face appeared softer somehow and a little more vulnerable. He didn't look quite so tough at the moment.

"That it is." He turned back to her, studying her face for a moment. "Night, Grace. Get some rest."

She moved toward the doorway of her cabin, unable to resist turning back one last time to wave at Boone as he revved his engine and disappeared down the lane.

As she settled in for the night a feeling of discomfort trickled through her. Boone had been so nice to come to her rescue this evening. Even though he'd been a bit prickly at first, he seemed like a good guy. It didn't feel great to make him believe she was in town as a participant in Operation Love. It felt like a lie. She shut her eyes tight and pressed her head against the pillow, determined to get a restful sleep.

One thought rattled around her brain as she drifted off to slumber. No one and nothing was going to get in her way of achieving her professional goals, not even a too-handsome-for-his-own-good sheriff who made her weak in the knees just by glancing in her direction.

Chapter Four

Grace woke up to a clanging sound resounding in her ears. For a moment a sense of disorientation hung over her like a heavy fog until she remembered—she was in Alaska! Bleary-eyed, she jammed her feet into her rabbit slippers, shuffled over to the front door and pulled it wide open. A gust of cold air blasted her in the face. A brilliant blue sky beckoned. Church bells were ringing!

When she crossed the threshold of her cabin, a slight rustling sound caught her attention. At her feet sat a pretty blue envelope, the color of a robin's egg. Her name jumped out at her in big bold letters. Grace picked up the envelope and brushed off the snow that had settled on top of it. Using her nail, she slit it open and took out the cream-colored card inside.

Grace,
If you're still interested in a tour of Love, I can pick you up at the Moose Café after your shift ends at two o'clock. If I don't hear from you, I'll assume you're game to explore…and hear about a legend or two.
Fondly,
Jasper Prescott

Yes! Score! She put the letter up to her lips and kissed it. A tour of Love would allow her to get an overview of the town she would be writing about. Although she'd done a little research prior to coming to town, there was nothing more invigorating than going out in the field and experiencing it for herself. Since Jasper Prescott was the one who'd coined the phrase *Operation Love* and written the original article about this lovelorn town, she considered it serendipity that he would be the one to show her around. It would be an added bonus if he told her about the legend. That would certainly give her something to write about!

Standing out on the porch in her robe and pj's felt surreal. Shivering, she looked around her, half expecting to see Primrose scampering through the brush. It was an incredibly beautiful vista. Huge mountains dominated the horizon. It almost felt as if she could reach out and touch them. She breathed in the fresh, pristine air, noticing for the first time that she had a partial view of the bay. The clouds sat in the sky like fluffy cotton balls. Everything felt so crisp and clean.

Grace threw back her head and extended her arms in the air. "Hello, world," she cried out, half expecting to hear an echo bounce back at her. It was the oddest feeling to be standing on her porch in Love, Alaska, communing with nature. Odd, yet refreshing at the same time. She hadn't expected to feel this rush of excitement thrumming through her veins. Truthfully, she hadn't been all that intrigued by Alaska, although she'd jumped at the opportunity to be entrusted with this series. It was quite a professional coup. Nevertheless, the forty-ninth state had never been on her list of places to visit, nor had she been aware of all its charm and raw beauty.

She always felt a burst of adrenaline whenever she began laying the groundwork for a story. Being here in Love, Alaska—a world far removed from what she was used to—heightened the thrill of it all. It made the normal challenges of her profession that much more difficult. And that much more exciting.

Grace's love of journalism had been sparked at the age of nine by her grandfather. Fred Corbett had been a businessman with a seat on the New York Stock Exchange. While he was ruthless in the boardroom, he was a teddy bear with his only granddaughter. Every time Grace visited his penthouse apartment on the Upper East Side, he'd asked her to bring him the newspaper from the foyer table. Dutifully, each and every time, Grace had brought him the furled copy of the *New York Tribune*.

"Read me the headlines, Gracie. Tell me what's going on in the world today," he'd instructed her in his signature booming voice. He'd sat back in his velvet-cushioned chair, closed his eyes and waited for her to begin.

Grace had read her grandfather the *Tribune*'s headlines and, in the process, fallen in love with the written word and the stories that made the world go round. Some of the stories made her want to cry, while others educated her about politics and global issues.

Wonderful job, Gracie. Knowing about the world around you is a powerful thing. Thanks for bringing the world to my doorstep today.

Her grandfather's praise had felt as warm as summer sunshine on her face. He'd made her feel like the most important person in the world, if only for those few minutes she'd held the newspaper in her hands and read aloud to him. It had been the first time in her life anyone had made her feel important. From that point forward she'd devoured the daily newspaper the way some kids gobbled down candy. The stories she uncovered between the pages of the newspaper served as fuel for her dreams. And she'd never forgotten the feeling of having the world at her fingertips. Moving hearts and minds with the power of her words never failed to amaze her.

At the sound of a door being opened, Grace turned toward Sophie's cabin. "Morning, Grace. It's our official first day of work. I'm so tickled. I could barely sleep last night." Sophie crossed her hands prayerfully, the same way Grace had done on Christmas morning when she was a child.

Bless her. Perhaps Sophie's enthusiasm about working at the Moose Café would rub off on her.

She waved at her new friend. "Hey, Sophie. Isn't the view beautiful?"

Sophie vigorously nodded her head. "It's almost as pretty as the bluebirds back in Saskell." Grace smiled. It was surprising Sophie had left Saskell in the first place. Every time she mentioned her hometown, Sophie lit up like the Fourth of July. What had made her come all the way to Alaska? She was the most lovable woman in the world. And beautiful. Surely she could have found love in Saskell, Georgia?

Not for the first time, Grace wondered why Sophie looked so familiar to her. As a journalist, she had a great memory for faces. This feeling of recognition wouldn't go away. It had been nagging at her since the flight over from Anchorage.

"Sophie, have we met before? Perhaps back in New York?"

Sophie's eyes widened. "N-no, ma'am. I don't think so. I didn't live in New York for long."

"Not a fan of big cities?" she asked. She was having a hard time picturing Sophie living in New York. She seemed like a country girl at heart. A real Georgia peach.

"I enjoyed visiting the Big Apple, but my heart never found a home there," Sophie said, her voice sounding wistful.

Hmm. Grace supposed she had her answer right there. Sophie's heart was looking for a home, and she'd come to Love in pursuit of it. Not surprisingly, Sophie's motives were way more noble than her own. She brushed that thought aside. There was no way she was going to let that knowledge eat at her.

After joining Hazel for blueberry pancakes and scrambled eggs at the Lodge, they headed to work at the Moose Café, with Hazel again at the wheel. It had snowed overnight, and as Grace looked around at her surroundings, she felt as if she was living in a true winter wonderland.

They'd barely stepped through the café's door before Cameron was handing out schedules and giving them each an additional uniform. Grace raised an eyebrow at the image of two moose kissing surrounded by a big red heart. She didn't know what vibe Cameron was aiming for, but this T-shirt resembled something a teenager might wear.

Cameron rubbed his hands together. He looked as if he was about to jump out of his skin. "Okay. Let's hit the ground running today." He looked back and forth between them. "Sophie, why don't you take the orders and act as hostess while Grace makes the drinks? Some customers just come in for regular coffee and pastries, so be ready to fill up cups, Sophie. Grace, we already have a customer looking for a mochaccino. I'll head back to the kitchen with Hazel and prepare the food."

"Yes, indeed. Sounds like a plan," Grace said, trying to make her voice sound as upbeat as Sophie's. *Fake it till you make it.* That was her motto.

"Here, Grace." Cameron handed her two slips of paper. "Hank comes in early for drinks to bring over to the firehouse. Extra whip on 'em, okay?"

"Got it!" Grace said, looking down at the slips for confirmation of the orders. One mochaccino. Four iced caramel macchiatos. Extra whipped cream.

She let out a sigh. It could have been much worse. At least it was the same drink times four. All she had to do was make two batches of caramel macchiato and serve 'em up in to-go cups. Then one batch of the mocha. There was a cheat sheet on the counter detailing all the ingredients in the most popular drinks. *Thank You, God.*

Everything stilled around her for a moment. It had been a long time since she'd thanked God for something. Matter of fact, before arriving in Love, she hadn't thought about God at all for a very long time. They were at a stalemate. In her darkest hours He hadn't answered her prayers, so she'd decided to ignore Him in return.

"You can do this, Grace," she said out loud, deciding on positive affirmations to get her through this situation.

One by one she assembled the items and placed them in the blender. Grace stared at the contents she'd placed inside. *Okay, this wasn't so bad after all.* It had never been her strong suit, but it wasn't rocket science. She might be a little slow putting all the ingredients together, but this was looking good. Chewing her lip, she considered all the buttons on the blender, finally deciding to push the biggest one. Nothing. She waited a few beats and pressed again. *Why wasn't this thing working?*

She bit her lip as she studied the machine. It wasn't

that different from the ones she'd used at Java Giant. Maybe a few more bells and whistles, but it had been four years since she'd worked for them. No doubt technology had advanced since then.

"Everything okay back here?"

The sound of Boone's husky voice swept over her like a strong gust of wind. She wanted to let out a loud groan. Of course! It would have to be Boone of all people to discover her in a state of utter confusion. What was he doing here anyway? The crime rate must be pretty low in this town if he could hang out so regularly at his brother's establishment.

"Just figuring things out," she said in an upbeat voice. She turned her head to look at him, her insides fluttering at the sight of Boone in his crisp uniform. If she ever got arrested, it just might take the sting out of it if the arresting officer looked half as good as Boone did.

She turned back toward the machine and pressed the black button. Nothing. Again she pressed it, tapping her foot with impatience when nothing happened. A hint of embarrassment trickled through her. She didn't want Boone to think she didn't know what she was doing. Gulp. Even if it was the truth.

Boone leaned in so that he was peering over her shoulder. The scent of sandalwood rose to her nostrils. His shoulder grazed against her arm, causing her equilibrium to shatter.

"Um, Grace. You might want to plug it in first."

Duh. She hadn't even plugged it in.

Way to make yourself look like a novice, Grace.

With a sheepish look in Boone's direction, she mumbled a thank-you and plugged the machine into the wall socket. A grinding noise rent the air as liquid began flying all over the place. She cried out as sprays of frosty macchiato blasted her in the face. Long arms reached in front of her and pressed the off button. Through the haze of slush on her eyelashes she watched as Boone grabbed a towel and began blotting her face with it.

"This is some first day of work," she said in a flippant voice. Hopefully, she'd hidden her mortification from Boone.

Boone drew his eyebrows together and frowned at her. "Something tells me you're no barista. Is this your first time?" His voice had a gruff edge.

"No," she said in a small voice. "I've done this dozens of times. I just never got the hang of it before I quit."

Boone raised an eyebrow. "Does Cameron know that?"

She bit down on her lip. Judging by the expression on Boone's face, there was no other choice but to fess up. "Not really. When I applied for this job I might have slightly exaggerated my skills." She sent him a pleading look. "And please don't tell him. I need this position."

His eyes narrowed. "You really want to be here, don't you?" The corners of his mouth relaxed into the hint of a smile.

"Yes. I need to be here." She was telling the truth. Being here in Love was paramount to digging up the information she needed for her series. Otherwise, it would be a puff piece. She didn't do puff pieces!

Boone shifted from one foot to the other. "I don't like keeping information from my brother. It's not my way of doing things. But I also realize how difficult it must be to start a new life in a place where everything is a world apart from what you're used to." He narrowed his eyes and studied her. "I won't say anything."

"Thank you," she gushed, feeling as if a huge weight had been lifted off her shoulders.

"I give you a lot of credit for uprooting your life in New York and coming here."

Their gazes locked and held. It felt as if the ground was moving underneath her feet. Instinctively, she reached for the wooden counter to steady herself.

"What happened back here?" Suddenly, Cameron was standing in the doorway, a deep frown marring his features.

Grace took a step away from Boone. The last thing she wanted her boss to think was that she was getting overly familiar with his brother. "I didn't mean to make a—" She began.

"It was my fault," Boone interrupted. His voice sounded matter of fact and smooth as butter. "I leaned in too close and got clumsy."

Cameron focused his gaze on Boone. Something unspoken flared between them.

"Perhaps you should be making your way back to the sheriff's office so Grace can get back to work." With a shake of his head, Cameron walked out of the room.

"You didn't have to do that," Grace said. "It's not worth Cameron being upset with you." She wasn't used to men swooping in to protect her. It made her feel all warm and fuzzy inside.

Boone shrugged. "It's no big deal. These days, we seem to be at odds with each other most of the time anyway."

Even though Boone was shrugging it off, she detected a hint of sorrow underneath the bravado. She'd been estranged from her own family for quite some time, and she knew how painful it was to deal with family issues.

"So," Grace said, forcing herself to focus on the matter at hand. "Any idea how this thing works?"

He nodded, causing a warm, comfortable feeling to settle over her. Boone moved closer toward her, quickly swallowing up the distance between them. "First, you have to make sure the top is tightly in place, like this. Sometimes if it doesn't latch on you're going to get a face full of goop." Boone placed his hand over hers on the blender. The feel of his warm, strong hand on top of her own was comforting. For a woman who'd been doing everything for herself for most of her adult life, it felt nice to have someone else take charge. It felt reassuring.

She looked up at him, sucking in a sharp breath at his close proximity. "I'm impressed that you know how to work this."

He shrugged, causing the fabric of his shirt to tighten against his muscular chest. She had to force herself to look away and focus on the machine.

"I've seen Cameron do it a few hundred times, give or take," he explained. "I'm good with gadgets."

For what felt like the hundredth time this morning, she shifted from one foot to the other. Standing on her feet all day was going to be a challenge in these heels. She was used to sitting at a desk for most of the day.

Boone looked down at her feet, his expression turning stern.

"How are your feet doing?"

"They're great," she said.

She looked down at her nude-colored shoes. They'd been killing her for the past hour straight, but she wasn't going to admit it. She let out a little sigh. It was such a shame. Shoes were her thing, especially these ones. Tagaros. The little wings on the soles were the signature of the designer. She'd scrimped and saved for weeks in order to buy them at full price. There were only four hundred of them in the world. But they were not the type of shoes a person could wear for a job that entailed standing on one's feet for most of the day.

"Actually, not so good," she admitted. The words slipped out of her mouth before she could rein them back in. She didn't feel like hearing an I-told-you-so from Boone.

Boone studied her face. His expression softened. "Talk to Hazel about her boots. She'll make sure you have a pair to work in and walk around town in."

Hazel's boots? She didn't need to borrow any boots from Hazel. She'd brought a few pairs with her, although she hadn't envisioned wearing them all day at work. Most of them had heels. With a woeful smile and a wave, Boone was gone. Although she should have been happy to get back to conquering the blender without an audience, she keenly felt the sheriff's absence. Much like warmth from the sun, he'd brightened up the small area with his rugged presence, leaving it in shadow once he departed.

Ever since Grace had admitted she wasn't a skilled barista, Boone's warning signs had been on high alert. There was something about Grace Corbett that just didn't compute. It had nagged at him ever since she'd stepped off the seaplane. Every instinct he'd honed during his tenure as town sheriff reinforced it. Not even those big sooty eyelashes of hers could distract him from his suspicions.

She'd lied on her application. If she was a barista, he was a ballerina. He wasn't a man who tolerated lies or the folks who told them. Why should he make an exception for her? And yet he'd agreed not to tell Cameron about her fudged résumé. Had that been a mistake?

Once bitten, twice shy. He'd learned his lesson years ago about women who couldn't tell the truth. Diana had taught him well. But he considered himself a fair man, and he knew it would be wrong to judge Grace based on another woman's actions.

Boone drained the last of his green tea from his mug and pushed himself away from the table. A quick glance at his watch confirmed that he needed to get back to the sheriff's office. For some reason he couldn't get the sight of Grace out of his mind. Her wide, blue eyes. The slushy coffee that had blanketed her hair and face... Those pink, kissable lips. All he wanted to do was grin from ear to ear.

"Mind telling me what you think you're doing?" Cameron stood in front of him with his arms folded across his chest. He was rocking back on his heels. His eyes flashed a warning sign.

"What? I'm a paying customer just like everyone else in here." Boone held up his receipt.

Cameron raised an eyebrow. "I don't recall you ever coming in here with such frequency, nor do I recall seeing you in the kitchen helping out my employees. If I remember correctly, you didn't think I should even open this place."

Boone gritted his teeth. "Hey, don't make me the bad guy here, Cam. I've been supportive in my own way."

Cameron scoffed. "How can you be the bad guy when I've already filled that role?"

"Gimme a break. I've never rubbed it in your face. I've spent the past year and a half defending you to everyone in town who accused you of leading with your heart instead of your head. I went above and beyond to help you out of the mess you made of the cannery deal."

Cameron's expression hardened "Never rubbed my face in it? Really? 'Cause it kind of feels like you just did."

Cameron stalked away with his fists at his side. Boone's heart sank, landing with a thud low in his gut. He hated being at odds with his brother. His siblings meant the world to him. Cameron, Liam and Honor. He loved all three of them with a single-minded devotion. As the oldest, it had always been his job to protect them from the slings and arrows of life. Even though he'd tried his best, he hadn't been able to rescue Cameron from becoming the town's whipping boy.

And ever since then there had been tension between them. As town sheriff, he'd been torn between his duties as a town official and his immense love for his brother. He'd always tilted in Cameron's favor, but his brother hadn't seen it that way. Cameron had felt like the town pariah. He let out a sigh as he walked back across the street to his office. The laid-back mood he'd experienced while in Grace's presence had evaporated like light fog on a summer morning.

Perhaps from now on he needed to steer clear of the Moose Café, even though the very thought of not seeing a certain blue-eyed girl left him feeling forlorn.

Grace had tried hard not to stare as Boone and Cameron faced off in the entryway to the Moose Café. She couldn't hear what they were saying, but their body language spoke volumes. Cameron had looked angry and tense, while Boone had seemed as if his patience was being tested. Tension had simmered in the air, and it felt almost explosive.

"What's up between those two?" she asked Hazel once the two had parted ways.

"There aren't enough hours in the day for me to explain," Hazel quipped. "Those two boys love each other, but sometimes the past can create wedges between people."

Wedges. Sounded like her family. Only there were wide crevasses in the Corbett family. Yet everyone pretended not to notice.

For the next few hours, Grace barely had time to focus on anything other than serving customers and trying to learn the ropes of her new job. Her mind was racing with unanswered questions as she filled orders and helped Hazel in the kitchen.

As they worked side by side, Grace enjoyed the easy camaraderie that flowed between them.

Hazel turned toward her with a pleased expression on her face. "I'm really happy that Cameron hired you and Sophie. There's a different energy in this place now that you're working here. You've brightened up the place."

Grace smiled. "Thanks, Hazel. That's sweet of you to say."

"I'm simply speaking the truth. And I haven't been sweet since I was knee-high to a grasshopper," she said with a laugh.

Grace frowned. "Hazel, if this town is having financial problems and the cannery closed, why were there two barista positions still available?"

Hazel made a face. "Well, the town's not broke. Not yet, anyway. This café is flourishing. Let's just say Cameron isn't the easiest person to work for. He's fired about two dozen people and the rest wouldn't work for him, not after—" Hazel clammed up.

"After what?" Grace asked.

Hazel slapped her hand to her forehead. "Me and my big mouth." She let out a sigh. "Cameron was handling the cannery deal for the town. The man he was doing business with took the town's money and headed out of Dodge." She shook her head mournfully. "Poor thing was trying to do a good thing for the town, but he got in way over his head. Not to mention his heart. Let's just say that a lot of people blame him for the whole thing falling apart."

"And it led to problems between him and Boone. Am I right?"

"I've already said too much, Grace." Hazel made a turning-the-key motion on her lips.

Cameron Prescott had been involved with an unscrupulous businessman, leading to the closing of the cannery. The soured deal had severely impacted the town. With his brother being the town sheriff, that had to have led to tension and discord.

Perhaps this community wasn't as tight-knit as she'd believed. Rifts between brothers. Unsavory businessmen. A town being fleeced.

Her journalistic juices were now flowing. Boone was at odds with his brother. Not to mention the townsfolk holding Cameron accountable. What kind of mistake could have turned so many people against Cameron? Whatever had transpired, she had an obligation to find out in order to write a comprehensive series about Love. Her series on this lovelorn town would be precise. No stone would remain unturned in her pursuit of the truth.

This wasn't going to be a fluff piece where she raved about the pretty mountains and the pristine air.

Hazel's face lit up like the Fourth of July. "Jasper! I wasn't expecting to see you today."

"I'm here on town business involving Grace." He wagged his eyebrows. "Official town business," Jasper affirmed.

Cameron's mouth quirked. "Town business? Grace is new in town. What kind of town business could it be?"

"Jasper wants to give me a personal tour of town," Grace piped up. "And maybe go legend hunting, right?"

Too late, she saw Jasper place a finger to his lips and give her a warning look.

Cameron and Hazel let out a groan in unison. Sophie's eyes went wide.

"Jasper," Hazel said in a warning tone. "There's a storm brewing for this evening. Don't get carried away out there."

Jasper snorted. "I know this town like the back of my hand! We'll only be gone for an hour or so." He glanced at his watch. "I have a meeting later on that I need to be back for."

"Well then, enjoy your tour," Hazel said with a sigh. "Grace, I'm glad I gave you a pair of my boots. They come in handy in this neck of the woods."

Grace felt sincerely grateful for Hazel's kindness. "Your boots will keep my toes nice and warm," Grace said. "Thanks again, Hazel. It's mighty generous of you." Grace looked down at the stylish, fur-lined boots—they were the most comfy boots she'd ever worn. And Hazel— dear, sweet woman—had given them to her earlier this morning out of the kindness of her heart. She'd had to force Hazel to take payment for the boots she'd designed and created, even though she'd protested at first. Grace had given her the same amount she would have paid for boots of this caliber if she'd found them in a big city. She wasn't sure Hazel knew the value of her product.

Hazel looked pleased at the compliment. "You're good advertising for my boots. If a beautiful city girl like yourself wears them, it might inspire everyone in town to buy a pair. Still got a few holdouts." She stared pointedly at Cameron, who studiously ignored her.

"You two have a great time," Sophie said with a wave.

Although Grace appreciated the sentiment, having a good time with Jasper was the last thing on her mind. Tony would expect at least a rough draft of her first article by the end of the week, and she intended to deliver the goods. After all, she'd come to Love in pursuit of a compelling story, not to make friends with an adorable, adventure-seeking senior citizen. Hazel had slipped earlier and given her some juicy details about the cannery deal, information she could definitely use in her series. And she wasn't letting up until she had everything she needed to make this series shine, even if she had to reveal a few closely guarded town secrets in the process.

Chapter Five

An hour later Jasper had shown Grace only a small portion of the town. He'd introduced her to every shopkeeper on Jarvis Street. Jasper drove her down to the bay where all the fishing boats were docked. He showed her the fishing vessels and explained how the town's economy was tied in to the fishermen and their catch. As Jasper explained it, the town of Love was known for producing top-quality pollack, salmon, halibut and cod. According to Jasper, locals had been making a living from the sea for hundreds of years.

Jasper also took her to the site of the cannery that had never come to pass. He appeared to be very emotional about the situation.

"We were standing on the precipice of something wonderful, something that would have been a game changer for this town," Jasper said. "But greed ruined everything."

Seeing the desolate look in his eyes caused an ache deep inside her. "I'm sorry, Jasper. It's hard to have something you were counting on snatched right out from under you."

It seemed that everyone they came across had a word or two for the town mayor. And they seemed just as excited to make her acquaintance. A woman named Dulcie tried to set her up on a date with her son. Thankfully, Jasper intervened and made a comment about how he was saving her for one of his grandsons. While Grace laughed nervously, Jasper didn't crack a smile, which led her to believe he may have been serious.

"Anything in particular you want to ask me about?" Jasper asked as he drove her away from the dock.

"I have to admit, I'm very curious about the town legend."

Jasper's eyes lit up. He reached out and patted her on the knee with his right hand, keeping the left one on the wheel. "Thatta girl, Grace. If you ask me, it's one of the most interesting things about this town."

Grace rubbed her mittens together. "Start at the beginning and don't leave anything out," she said in an excited voice. It was thrilling to imagine actual treasure being buried here in town.

"My great-great-grandfather, Bodine Prescott struck gold in the Gold Rush. While everybody and their brother headed to the Yukon, Bodine struck gold in Juneau, Alaska. According to family lore, he was one of the first who hit pay dirt. When he came back to Love everyone wanted a piece of what he'd found." He shook his head. "He couldn't trust a soul, so he hid the gold somewhere in Love while he tried to sort everything out."

"And he never went back to retrieve it?" Grace asked.

"He drowned out on the Bay with his brother, Jack, not too long after his return. It was a tragic loss of life. Two women lost their husbands, and their children were now fatherless. When his wife, Sadie, went through his belongings, she found some notes he'd left in a journal. In it, Bodine talked about his discovery and laid down some hints as to where he'd stashed it. Although they tried to locate it, none of them were successful. 'Rivers of gold' was the biggest hint, which has always made me think of the limestone cave since a river runs through the Nottingham Woods."

"I can see why you're so intrigued by this," Grace murmured. Jasper had created such a vivid picture in her mind of the events back in the late eighteen hundreds. She'd always found the Gold Rush such an interesting topic.

"Are you game to check the cave?" Jasper's expression radiated enthusiasm. His blue eyes twinkled with a hint of mischief.

"Of course," she said, jumping at the chance to do something outside of the box. "But I thought you had a meeting to attend."

Jasper waved his hand dismissively. "It's just an appointment to get my hair cut. I'd rather go spelunking with you. They say there's snow coming later on tonight, so let's get moving."

Spelunking! It wasn't on her bucket list of things to do, but she felt a trickle of excitement dancing along her spine as Jasper made a U-turn in the road and headed in the direction of the woods. This would definitely be something worth writing about in her article.

Nottingham Woods was located about twenty minutes from the center of town. The area of Love they traveled through to get there was sparsely populated. They drove endless stretches of road with nothing more than trees, a never-ending amount of snow and moose-crossing signs.

Grace cried out as a large moose sauntered across the

road. Jasper seemed to have almost anticipated it since he slowed the car down about twenty feet away from the moose.

Jasper appeared tickled by her reaction. "Don't worry, Grace. We're used to moose sightings in these parts, which is why we don't speed on these roads. Hitting a moose could land you in the emergency room. Nothing to worry about though."

Grace took out her phone and began snapping pictures. "I can't believe it! I was beginning to think these moose sightings were make-believe."

The sound of Jasper's rumbling laughter filled the silence in the car. "I told you Alaska was about discovery."

They were now really and truly in the Alaskan wilderness. Although they'd passed a few homes in the past few miles, not a single car traveled the road with them. A huge cedar sign heralded their arrival at the woods as soon as they reached their destination. After stepping outside of the car, Grace sucked in a breath as the awesome sight of the mountains jumped out at her. The view was stunning, almost like something from a postcard. No doubt it would say something like, "Welcome to Love" over a photo of the spectacular mountain.

As she trailed behind Jasper, she looked around at her surroundings. Nothing but trees dusted in white, an abundance of snow at every turn and miles of forest. Everything looked the same. She was glad Jasper knew the route so well. When they reached a fork in the woods, Jasper abruptly turned right. As she fought to keep up with his pace, she couldn't help but think he moved pretty spryly for a man in his seventies. After a ten-minute trek in the snow, Jasper stopped in his tracks and pointed to a cave. It had been partially covered with tree limbs, but there was a gap where a person could easily gain entrance.

Grace wrinkled her nose. She wasn't sure if this was a good idea after all. "I-is it safe, Jasper? How do you know there aren't any wild animals in there? Or spiders?"

"We don't. That's part of the adventure."

Grace took a step backward. Adventure was one thing. She'd already gotten up close and personal with Primrose. A de-scented skunk was as close as she was getting to wild animals. And she planned to run all the way back to town if she saw a single creepy crawling spider.

Jasper threw back his head and clutched his belly with laughter. "Just teasing you, Grace. The animals in these parts aren't cave dwellers. And the bats only come out at night."

Ewww. Bats?

At least it was only four o'clock or so. Surely she and Jasper wouldn't be hanging out until it got dark. He was going to show her the area where he thought the gold might be buried. They'd be long gone by the time the bats came out to play.

Jasper walked into the cave and turned around to wave her in.

Grace caught up to Jasper and walked right behind him as he entered the cave. Once inside, she struggled to see the dark interior. Only a sliver of light trickled in from outside.

Jasper angled his flashlight toward the cave ceiling about twenty feet away. "That's limestone back there. See right there where the roof is shimmering?"

Grace craned her neck to get a glimpse of the yellowish limestone. Jasper's flashlight illuminated the area, showcasing an almost iridescent stone.

"Wow. It's practically glowing." Yellow or not, Grace felt that the odds of finding treasure in this immense cave were slim to none. Matter of fact, the whole legend was beginning to sound bogus.

"Let's get a closer look," Jasper suggested, just as he stumbled and went down like a ton of bricks. He landed with a thud.

"Jasper? Are you all right?" Grace's cry seemed to bounce off the walls and echo in the silence.

"I'm fine. Just tripped over this rock. These eyes of mine aren't as sharp as they used to be."

"Let me help you up." She bent over and grasped Jasper by the wrist. Gently, she pulled him up. Halfway, Jasper winced and cried out in pain. He sank back down to the cave floor.

"My ankle. I can't seem to put any weight on it."

"Why don't I put my arm around you and help you walk."

Jasper frowned. "Grace, I don't think that's going to work. I'd topple you over. I think it might be broken."

She watched as Jasper grimaced and pulled down his sock. His ankle was red and swollen. There was no way he was walking anywhere on it. Their lighthearted adventure had suddenly turned serious. It would be getting dark outside soon due to the shorter days this time of year.

"I'm calling for help." Grace bit her lip as she took out her phone from her pocket and looked for a signal on her phone. No reception! She looked around the cave, half expecting an answer to their dilemma to come out of nowhere.

"I can't get any reception, Jasper. I think that I need to go get someone to help us." With Jasper's ankle out of commission and no cell service, their choices were pretty limited. Turning into a Popsicle out here in the wilderness wasn't an option. There was no time to waste.

"This is all my fault. I'm so sorry our adventure turned out this way." Jasper's head hung down in a dejected fashion.

"Are you kidding me?" Grace said with a cheery smile and false bravado. "I always wanted to rescue someone. Now's my opportunity." *Unless of course she fell into a snowy ravine or was eaten by a polar bear.*

"Let me help you get oriented. When you head out of the cave go straight until you get to the fork. Take a left at the fork and keep walking until you see the tree with the twisted branches. Turn right at the tree and then head straight down the slope. You'll run right into the area where my truck is parked. The keys are inside. Just take it nice and easy on the road if you can't get a signal. There's a house a few miles down the road by the entrance to the mountain." Jasper began to rummage around in his side pocket. He pulled out a pair of mittens. "Take these. It will give you an extra layer of protection."

Grace reached for the mittens and put them on over her own pair. "Will you be all right by yourself?" She hated leaving him all alone in this desolate cave.

"I'll be fine. And I'm not by myself. God is by my side. The Lord is my rock, my fortress and my savior."

"I'll be back in a flash," she said, zipping up her coat all the way to her neck before she stepped outside the cave.

She traveled in a straight line, following the path they'd previously traveled. Jasper was counting on her and she wasn't going to let him down.

Lord, please show me the way. Guide me out of this forest.

When she arrived at the fork, she tried to remember exactly what Jasper had told her. There was a feeling of panic rising up inside her. She couldn't think straight. Right, left or maybe straight. Which way? She really had no idea. She should go back to the cave! Turning around, she realized there were several different paths to choose from. And she had not a single idea of which way to go. Now she was really and truly lost. And it was starting to snow. Big, huge snowflakes were falling from the gray sky. One landed on the tip of her nose. If she was safely inside her cabin with a big mug of hot chocolate, she might find them beautiful. Now they just seemed like obstacles to finding her way out of this forest.

Grace didn't feel brave anymore. Not by a long shot! Fear had nestled its way right into her bones. She was frozen right down to her pinky toes.

This wasn't a grand adventure anymore. It was cold out here—mind-numbingly cold—and she wasn't exactly dressed to sleep out in the elements. This trek was supposed to be a short tour of the caves, a fun excursion that would give her some interesting fodder for her articles. Spelunking, Jasper had called it. For a city girl like herself, spelunking had sounded like a journalist's dream. An adventure to recount in her golden years. Now, it had all the earmarks of a nightmare.

She brushed snow off a nearby log and sat down on it. She looked furtively around the clearing. *Lions, tigers and bears. Oh, my!* The thought ran through her mind. Even though she knew there might not be tigers in Alaska, she was pretty sure that bears and mountain lions freely roamed the tundra.

Please, Lord. Don't let a wild animal mistake me for a snack. Please let me find my way out of this mess.

Tears pricked at her eyes. This wasn't looking good. Not only had she sealed her own fate by venturing out on her own, but she'd left Jasper back in the cave all by his lonesome with a bum ankle. He was depending on her to get help. Maybe this was her just desert for poking her nose around in Love and for pretending that she was in town as a participant in Operation Love.

Thoughts of her family raced through her mind. What would her parents think if she expired out here in the wilderness? She could just hear her father now. *"Never thought a child of mine would freeze to death in the wilds of Alaska. I told her that job of hers was a waste of time."*

She felt moisture on her cheeks, and it wasn't snowflakes melting on her skin. Tears. The fact that she was actually crying surprised her. She hadn't even cried when Trey had called off the wedding. Nor had she shed a single tear when she'd stood in front of a church full of guests and announced the shocking news that the ceremony wouldn't be taking place. Time and time again God had shown her that she wasn't His favored child. She wasn't worthy of His time or consideration. Her prayers were never answered.

Why should this time be any different?

Boone sighed as he riffled through the correspondence Shelly had placed on his desk. He sat up straight when his own handwriting jumped out at him. A big red stamp with the words *Return To Sender* had him heaving a great big sigh. The letter he'd addressed to Miss Honor Prescott hadn't even been opened. Pain threatened to crack him wide open. His sister was still mad at him for sending her away to get her education in the Lower 48. She still hadn't forgiven him for busting up her plans to

elope with her boyfriend three years ago. She'd only been nineteen at the time and in love with a man who wasn't worthy of her devotion. Ever since then she seemed to take pleasure in cutting him out of her life.

He shook his head, knowing if he had to do it all over again, he would make the same choices. Protecting his little sister had been his number-one goal. Perhaps, he realized, he could have handled it with a little more finesse. Maybe if he had, she wouldn't hate him like she did.

His intercom began to buzz, jolting him out of his thoughts. Shelley's voice came through loud and clear. "Sheriff Prescott, you have a visitor."

Before he could even respond, his office door burst open.

Grace's red-haired friend Sophie stood in the door-way, huffing and puffing as if she'd just run a marathon. "Sheriff Prescott. I've come down here to file a missing-persons report," she blurted out.

Boone had to stop himself from smirking. He was waiting for the punch line. Had Miss Sophie Miller lost a kitten? Or a press-on nail?

"It's my friend, Grace. I haven't seen her since this afternoon when she went on a tour with Mayor Prescott. She should have been back hours ago."

"A tour? Led by Jasper?" Boone folded his hands on his desk and lowered his head.

Sophie bit her lip. "Sheriff, you sound as worried as I feel."

Boone stood up from his desk and reached for his walkie-talkie, holster and gun. "No need to worry, Sophie. I know this town like the back of my hand. I'm going to find Grace and bring her back safe and sound. You can count on it."

* * *

Boone hadn't wasted a minute mobilizing the search-and-rescue team. Thankfully, Jasper was as predictable as the tides. Boone knew exactly where he'd taken Grace. The caves at Nottingham Woods were the one place Jasper couldn't resist showing anyone who was adventurous enough to accompany him.

Although for the life of him he couldn't imagine what had happened out there to prevent them from returning back to town hours ago. Boone had followed behind the search-and-rescue team in his cruiser, resisting the urge to speed. He'd been at the site of too many accidents not to realize the foolishness of speeding on snow and ice-slicked Alaskan back roads. If his truck ended up in a ditch, he wouldn't be any help at all to Grace and Jasper.

By the time they reached Nottingham Woods, the adrenaline was flowing like crazy through his veins. With the team following behind him, he led the way toward the caves since he knew the route like the back of his hand. He'd grown up in these woods—hiking, adventuring, spelunking with Jasper. Fear lodged in his throat at the very idea of Jasper and Grace being in trouble out here. These woods were deceptive. One wrong turn and you ended up deep in the interior with no idea how to find your way out.

It was a blessing the two of them were together. If nothing else, Jasper knew Nottingham Woods better than anyone in Love.

A glance down at the trail revealed no footprints in the snow. Since snowflakes had been falling for the past hour, they'd covered up any tracks he might have been able to detect. He called out to the search-and rescue team as soon as he spotted the caves. One glance at the disturbed branches in front of the cave told him that someone had been here. He prayed Jasper and Grace were still inside rather than wandering in the woods.

Boone stepped inside the cave, his eyes peeled for two figures in the dark. The yellowish glow from the limestone lent a slight amount of illumination to an otherwise pitch-black cave. He pointed his flashlight in all directions and called out in a booming voice, "Jasper. Grace. It's Boone." Out of the corner of his eye he spotted a flash of movement.

"Boone." The sound of Jasper's voice sounded as sweet as honey to his ears. "Here I am. Way over here."

He moved quickly toward Jasper, who was leaning against a cave wall with his leg propped up on a rock. His grandfather grimaced as he pulled up his pant leg. There was no question he was injured, judging by the red and swollen appearance of his ankle.

"Are you okay, Jasper?" Boone asked, crouching down so he was at eye level with his grandfather.

"I'm fine, Boone," Jasper answered. "My ankle just aches a bit and I'm a little chilled."

"Where's Grace?" Boone looked around the cave with his flashlight before turning back toward Jasper.

Jasper's eyes widened. "Grace? Isn't she with you? She went for help hours ago."

Hours ago? Everything went still for a moment as the implications of Jasper's statement sunk in. Grace, who had no knowledge of the Nottingham woods or the conditions out here, was all alone after leaving the caves to seek rescue. His throat went dry as he thought of all the various ways that this could end in disaster. Panic gripped him by the throat. Reminding himself to keep calm, he swallowed past the fear. Turning toward the search-and-rescue team, he said, "Grace Corbett is out here in the woods, presumably lost. She's been out in the elements for hours, and she's not familiar with this terrain or how rapidly the weather can change. We need to find her... as fast as we possibly can."

It was getting darker by the minute. A big fat moon hung in the sky. Stars began to fill the nighttime sky. And it felt even colder than it had five minutes ago, if that was possible. Although she was thankful for her two layers of mittens, her furry hat and her comfy down jacket, Hazel's fur-lined boots were the real blessing. She could still move her toes. But she was freezing. Her fingertips were beginning to ache, and she couldn't feel her face anymore, with the exception of her nose. It felt as if it had been wind burned.

How she wished she had a piece of paper and a pen. If she was going to meet her demise out here in the Alaskan wilderness, it would be nice to be able to write a goodbye letter. Perhaps she could pen one last column for the *Tribune*. "Alaska: The Final Frontier."

"Hello. Goodbye. From Alaska." She began to giggle at the ridiculousness of it all. None of her acquaintances in New York City would believe that she'd perished in Alaska in a town called Love.

"Grace! Grace!" Frostbite was setting in, as well as delusions. The sound of Boone's voice was now streaming into her consciousness. If she was going to perish out here she might has well have her last thoughts center around a scrumptious lawman. Too bad they'd never kissed. It would have been one memorable, earth-shattering kiss, she imagined.

She felt someone shaking her. Her eyes blinked open.

Boone. He was next to her, his dark chocolate eyes full of concern. "Grace! Are you all right? I need to get you out of here and see that you get checked out by a doctor."

"You're here. You're really here," she said as she reached out and pinched his arm through his jacket. "I thought I was seeing a mirage."

"You can thank Sophie later. She raised the alarm when you didn't return to the cabins."

Sophie had noticed she hadn't made it home. The very thought of her new friend hunting down law enforcement on her behalf made her chest tighten with emotion.

"Jasper! I left him in the cave when I went to find help." How could she have forgotten about poor, sweet Jasper?

"He's been found by the rescue team. He was sheltered from most of the elements by sitting in the cave right where you left him. He's beside himself with worry about you." His eyes flickered with emotion. "We all were."

"I never thought it would be so easy to get turned around," she said sheepishly. "Then I figured it was best to stay put so I wouldn't get even more lost."

"Can you feel your fingers and toes?"

"A little bit." She tried to wiggle them as a shooting pain speared through her fingers. "Ouch. That hurts. These boots saved my b-bacon." She felt a warm sensation on her cheek. There was a dog with Boone. And he was licking her. She nuzzled her face against his neck, appreciating the love fest.

"Kona! That's enough," Boone ordered, his voice stern and authoritative.

"No, Boone. He's fine." She turned toward Kona and nuzzled his head. "Thanks for helping to find me, Kona."

Boone pulled out a walkie-talkie and began to speak.

"Hank. I found her. I'm going to take her to be evaluated for hypothermia. Tell the team thanks for all the help. And make sure you let Sophie Miller know Grace has been found. She's staying up at the Black Bear Cabins."

A crackly voice came across the line. "That's good news, Boone. Jasper was taken to the clinic to see about his ankle. He's in good shape. I'll let him know about Grace."

"Thanks for the update." Boone signed off and placed the walkie-talkie back in his hip pocket.

"Let's get you out of here." Boone reached down and swung her up against his chest. Her face was so close to his she could see the copper colored flecks in his pupils.

Suddenly, she didn't feel half as cold as she had a few moments ago. There was a warmth spreading through her chest like wildfire.

"Boone. Thanks for rescuing me," she murmured. "I really appreciate it."

"You're welcome. It's the least I could do since my grandfather was the one who got you into this predicament."

The gruffness in his voice startled her. He wasn't warm and fuzzy in the slightest. He seemed…angry. Perhaps he was upset because town resources had been used to locate her. He'd mentioned a rescue team. Surely that wasn't cheap. And from everything she'd heard, Love was a town struggling to stay afloat.

She couldn't help but feel a little crushed. Steeling herself against the pain caused by Boone's behavior, she focused on getting back to a warm cabin and her comfy blankets. Investing herself in a temperamental town sheriff was dumb. And there were many things people might call her, but dumb wasn't one of them.

* * *

For most of his adult life, Boone had been firmly in control. Of his career. Of his siblings. And of his emotions. The one time he'd thrown caution to the wind and tumbled over the edge had been when he'd fallen in love with Diana. Although it had been an absolute train wreck, it taught him to listen to his inner voice. Something was telling him not to trust Grace. And he was now caught between a rock and a hard place because he liked her. He really, really liked Grace Corbett.

Suddenly, it felt as if he was out on that ledge again, teetering between safety and the danger zone.

When he'd realized Grace wasn't in the cave with Jasper he'd been in the grip of a gut-wrenching fear that had threatened to swallow him up whole. It hadn't let up on him until he'd spotted her sitting on the log with her eyes closed, as if she was an ice queen frozen in time. Joy had risen up inside him at the sight of her. And he didn't quite know how to process that wealth of feeling. It was making him feel a little cranky.

Lately, he'd felt as if God was testing him. All the relationships in his life were at a crossroads. Honor wasn't speaking to him. His brother Liam had holed himself up in a little bubble where nothing and no one could reach him. And his relationship with Cameron was still fractured. His grandfather seemed to have aged suddenly in the past few years, and he was scared of losing him.

And now, out of the blue, his heart was beginning to open up again. All because of Grace. Beautiful, mysterious Grace, who seemed as ill-suited to Love as he would be to the concrete, high-rise world she'd come from. But sometimes, he reckoned, the things that didn't seem to make sense were the very things that turned out to be wonderful.

When they reached the edge of the woods, he walked quickly over to his car and opened the door while holding Grace against him with his other arm. As soon as the door was open, he set her down in the front seat and buckled her up. He opened the back door for Kona and let out a whistle. Kona ran out of the woods and made a beeline for his car, jumping right inside.

After a few minutes of rummaging around in the truck, he settled himself into the driver's seat. He turned toward Grace and covered her up with a fleece blanket. Her teeth were chattering. He struggled against the impulse to cradle her in his arms and give her some of his body warmth. Getting her the medical attention she needed was his main priority.

"Cover yourself with this blanket. You'll warm up in a few minutes."

"W-where are we going?" she asked as she gazed out the window. No doubt she'd realized they weren't heading back in the direction of town.

Boone cast a quick glance in Grace's direction. Her lips were still a purplish hue, and she was shivering like crazy. He knew all too well that the frigid temperatures in Alaska could easily lead to hypothermia. He could head back to town and have Grace seen at the clinic, but he knew of a better, quicker solution.

"I'm taking you to get checked out by a doctor. He lives a few miles from here."

Grace frowned. "Way out here, so far from town?"

Boone nodded. "He's had a rough time of it lately. His wife was killed in an accident. He's raising his son all by himself and not practicing at the moment. But don't worry…he'll treat you."

"How can you be sure of that? It sounds like he wants to be left alone."

"He does want to be left alone, but I can't stand by and let that happen. A long time ago I vowed to take care of all my siblings, no matter what. He may be Dr. Liam Prescott, but he's still my little brother."

Chapter Six

A long time ago I vowed to take care of all my siblings, no matter what.

Just when she'd been about to write Boone off as a moody jerk, he went and said something that yanked at her heartstrings. This man was a protector, all the way down to his silver-tipped boots. What she wouldn't give to have her own brother feel that strongly about her. There wasn't a single memory she had of Brian protecting or caring for her. And she wasn't exaggerating in her belief that he didn't care whether she was in Alaska or Timbuktu or the Sahara.

Grace turned toward Boone, studying his strong face in profile. His rugged features were tense. A tiny vein thrummed above his eye while his hands were tightly gripping the steering wheel.

"Siblings? I assumed it was just you and Cameron. How many do you have?"

"Three. Cameron. Liam. And my sister, Honor." Boone kept his eyes focused on the road. The snow was coming down even faster now, and it seemed to be sticking.

"Honor," she said, wrapping the blanket ever tighter around her body. "That's a pretty name."

His expression softened. "It suits her. She just graduated from college last spring. She's working on her master's now in wildlife biology."

"Are you close?" Although she'd always wanted to have a tight relationship with her older brother, it had never materialized. She envied siblings who actually had warm feelings for one another and strong ties that bound them together.

A sigh slipped past his lips. "We used to be, before I sent her away to school in Minnesota. Now she'd rather eat glass than be in a room with me."

Boone's tone hinted at a sorrow he most likely kept hidden away from the world. She recognized it instantly. It existed right under the surface where it couldn't be seen. Seems they did have something in common after all.

"This, too, shall pass. She can't stay mad forever," Grace said. The sudden urge to comfort him surprised her.

Boone scoffed. "You don't know my sister. She thinks I stood in the way of her one true love." He made a clucking sound with his teeth. "That type of anger burns for a while."

The car slowed down as Boone turned into a private road lined on either side with huge spruce trees. Just as she was about to ask if they were close, a house appeared out of nowhere. The little log cabin nestled in the woods resembled something from a fairy tale. It looked tranquil and serene, as if nothing could touch it. Long icicles resembling daggers hung from the front porch. A soft light emanated from the window. There was no way of telling from the outside that tragedy had marred the lives of the occupants of this house. Everything looked so perfect.

Once he stopped the car, Boone quickly made his way over to the passenger side and helped her out of the vehicle. Grace stood a few steps behind Boone as he rapped on the door. Kona sat next to Boone wagging his tail. When no one came, he knocked again, this time more insistently.

The door opened with a flourish, providing a blast of warmth and light from inside the house. Instead of one Dr. Liam Prescott standing in the doorway, there was a young woman with long, chestnut-colored hair, gray-blue eyes and a sardonic expression on her face.

"Well, I guess the gig is up. Aren't you going to welcome me back to Alaska, big brother?"

Seeing his beautiful little sister positioned in the doorway of Liam's house caused a myriad of emotions to swirl around inside him. Disbelief. Joy. Curiosity. Anger.

"Honor?" Her name came out sounding like a question. Shock roared through him at the notion that his sister was actually here in Love. Why wasn't she in Minnesota? Why hadn't anyone told him she'd come home?

She tipped her head in his direction by way of greeting, even though he would rather have hugged it out. "Hi, Boone." Her eyes drifted toward Grace. "Why don't you come in? Your girlfriend looks frozen."

"She's not my girlfriend. Honor, this is Grace Corbett." He placed his hand on the small of Grace's back and gently guided her into the house. Kona followed dutifully behind him. There really wasn't any time for pleasantries. He scanned the immediate area for his brother. "Where's Liam? She needs to be checked for hypothermia."

Honor's eyes widened. "He's putting Aidan down for the night. I'll go get him." Honor hurried off down the corridor, stopping at the last door on the right. He watched as she gently turned the knob and entered.

"Aidan is my nephew," he explained. Just the thought of him caused his chest to tighten with emotion. His life had already been marred by loss at such a young age.

Boone turned toward Grace, eager to make her comfortable. "Grace, let me take your coat off." He unzipped her coat, noticing that her lips looked slightly less purple. She was still shivering.

"Come sit by the fire, and I'll get your boots off."

Grace sank down into an oversize love seat right next to the fire. He immediately began to take off her boots and socks. "I don't think I've ever been so happy to see a roaring fire." He watched as her lids began to get droopy. She could barely hold her head up.

"You can't go to sleep, Grace. That could be a sign of hypothermia," Boone warned her. Grace's lids flew open, and once again he found himself basking in the brilliance of her blue eyes.

He felt a sudden wave of anger toward his grandfather. *What in the world had gotten into Jasper?* This was all his fault. How could he have sent Grace to get help in a remote, wooded area she wasn't even familiar with? The whole situation had been a recipe for disaster! Things could have gotten much worse if Grace had wandered farther into the woods and toward the mountain.

Liam walked into the room, his stride full of purpose and a sense of urgency. He was in doctor mode at the moment. It would have made Boone smile, but for the fact he was still worried about Grace.

"Boone. What's going on? Honor said it was a medical emergency." His eyes swung over toward Grace.

"Liam, this is Grace Corbett. Grace here got lost in the woods this afternoon when she went spelunking with Jasper. She was out there for almost two hours before we were able to rescue her. I'm a little worried about how long she was exposed to the elements."

Liam walked over and crouched down so that he was on his haunches. He gave Grace one of his most endearing smiles. "Hi, Grace. I'm Liam. I'm going to check out your hands and toes for hypothermia, okay?"

Grace bobbed her head up and down. "Sounds good, Dr. Prescott."

"You can call me Liam," he said, peeling back Grace's sock to reveal toes that looked a bit gray. He began examining her feet and fingers, earning himself a few cries of pain from the patient.

He glanced back at Boone. "We're going to warm up her toes first. Go get a tub of warm water for me. There's a basin under the kitchen sink."

Boone did as Liam instructed and filled the basin almost to the top. When he returned to the living room, Grace was wrapped up in another blanket. He set the basin down in front of her, anxiously watching as she slipped her feet in the water. Grace let out a contented sigh as she did so.

"How's it looking?" he asked Liam.

"Pretty good considering the weather. I'd say she was very fortunate to have those boots, a heavily insulated coat and two layers of mittens. As it is, she probably has frostbite, but nothing that requires further medical attention. I'm going to continue to warm her body up slowly and put some bandages on her toes and fingers.

She's got a few blisters that might be uncomfortable for a few weeks."

"Are you sure?" Boone asked. "She was out there for a long time."

Liam narrowed his eyes at him. He studied him for a moment before he answered. "Of course I'm sure, unless you know something I don't."

Sensing the tension, Grace looked back and forth between the two of them.

Liam sighed, his broad shoulders heaving. "Is there something else you want to ask me?"

"How long has she been back?" Boone spit the question out, his voice bristling with anger.

Liam looked up at him, his blue eyes weary. "Two days ago she showed up at my front door saying she completed her master's degree early. Begged me not to call you."

Boone chewed the inside of his cheek. "Did Declan fly her in?"

The thought of his best friend being involved in this conspiracy unsettled him. He'd been tight with Declan since they were little kids, and if he'd done this behind his back, it would feel like a betrayal. That possibility hurt him more than he could ever put in to words.

"Stop grilling Liam. If you want to know the answers to any questions about me, then you can go straight to the source." Honor was standing at the threshold of the living room, her hands perched on her hips. A very familiar, defiant expression was etched on her face. "And for your information, it wasn't Declan who flew me into Love." She frowned. "He's not the only pilot in Alaska."

Relief flooded him. In the worst of times, he could always rely on Declan. When the Prescott family issues got too tangled, his best friend served as an excellent sounding board. He prayed it would never change.

"How long?" he spit out, his gaze focused on Honor.

"How long what?" Honor asked, her voice full of attitude.

"How long are you going to stay mad at me, 'cause this silent routine is getting really old."

Although her fingers, face and toes were coming back to life, Grace was beginning to think she should run and take cover. Boone versus Honor was proving to be an epic showdown. Liam just looked worn-out, as if he'd heard this same argument too many times to count. Although she'd been curious about Boone and his siblings, she now felt that she knew way more about their relationships than she wanted to know.

She wasn't taking sides, but she couldn't help but feel badly for Boone. All he wanted to do was keep watch over his three siblings. From where she was standing, he seemed mighty heroic.

"You've never once apologized for sandbagging my life," Honor shouted.

Boone's arms were folded across his chest. "I won't apologize for watching out for you."

Honor fisted her hands at her side and let out a little scream. "Watching out for me? Is that what you call it? You ruined my life."

Boone rolled his eyes. "That is so dramatic. I saved you from making the biggest mistake of your life." He scoffed. "Married at eighteen to an unemployed troublemaker? Not on my watch."

Liam shut his eyes and put his head in his hands. He muttered something unintelligible.

Honor pointed her finger at Boone. "You're just bitter because the woman you loved cheated on you! Don't take it out on me."

A shocked silence filled the air. Grace watched Boone's entire body go slack. He winced and shut his eyes for a brief moment. Grace looked down at her hands, swallowing past the hurt and embarrassment she felt on his behalf.

"Honor! That's enough," Liam said in a warning tone. He looked as if he might snap in two. From the first moment she'd seen Liam, there had been an air of sadness hovering over him like a shroud. Although he was cut from the same tall, dark and handsome mold as his brothers, there were dark shadows under his eyes and a look of utter defeat. He didn't need a battle breaking out in his own home while his child was sleeping nearby.

"The two of you might want to quiet down to a dull roar. There's a child sleeping down the hall." Grace's words drew both their attention. Honor frowned at her. Boone opened his mouth to say something but then shut it.

Liam shot her a grateful look. "Thanks, Grace. It's nice to know there's at least one other adult in the room."

A rustling noise drew all their attention to the doorway where a little boy with chubby cheeks stood, his thumb firmly rooted in his mouth as he looked around the room. He was wearing a pair of footed pajamas with a fire truck on it. His hair was disheveled. He seemed to be about three or four years old.

"Uncle Boone." Aidan padded his way over to Boone and held his hands straight up in the air.

Grace couldn't remember the last time she'd seen such an adorable child. With his curly dark hair and big eyes, Aidan was the spitting image of his father.

"Hey, buddy. How are you doing?" Boone asked as

he scooped up Aidan in his arms and rocked him side to side.

Grace felt a little short of breath as she watched Boone nuzzle his face into his nephew's neck. Aidan's tinkling laughter rang out in the room. *Leave it to the kid to lighten the mood.* His joy served to diffuse the anger and acrimony that had bubbled over like an overfilled pot.

Aidan tugged on Boone's chin. "I love you, Uncle Boone."

Grace felt a well of emotion building up inside her. This little boy had lost his mother not that long ago, and the thought of this sweet munchkin not having a mother to tuck him in at night brought tears to her eyes.

"I love you, too, Aidan," Boone said in a voice laden with emotion.

"It's night-night time, A-man," Liam said, his voice tender and paternal.

"I'll put him down," Honor said. She quickly moved toward Boone, who smoothly transferred Aidan into her arms. Something unspoken happened between the siblings. Their eyes met and there seemed to be some recognition that they'd both crossed a line. Boone reached out and ruffled Honor's hair. She smiled at him, tears and regret shining in her eyes.

Grace didn't know if it was because her feet were resting in tepid water, the blazingfire in the hearth or the wool blanket wrapped around her body, but she suddenly felt all warm and fuzzy inside.

Despite the conflict between Boone and his sister, it was obvious that there was a lot of love in this room. It practically bounced off the walls. It hummed and buzzed in the moments of silence. It radiated in a child's unbridled laughter. From what she'd learned so far about the Prescott family, there were fissures and cracks in its foundation. But, unlike her own family, they were still connected, still invested in one another. Still fighting the good fight. At the end of the day, that's what it was all about.

It was almost ten o'clock by the time Boone got on the road with Grace to head back to town. Liam had bandaged Grace's fingers and toes. The four of them had sat down together to a dinner of Liam's chili and corn bread. It had been nice to sit down as a family and show Grace that they weren't just bickering fools. He wasn't sure why, but he cared deeply about how she viewed the Prescott family.

The snow had been steadily falling for the past few hours. The road was slick and packed with snow. The trek back to town would be slow going, but he was used to driving in blizzard-like conditions. A little snow didn't scare him. He wasn't so sure about Grace. She was unusually quiet, and she kept peering out the window at the snowflakes whirling.

"I owe you an apology." He let out a sigh. Those words had been sitting on his chest for the past few hours. He figured he might as well get them out of the way.

Grace wrinkled her nose. "An apology? For what? If it hadn't been for you, I might be a frozen Popsicle by now."

He felt his lips twitching. Leave it to Grace to make him want to laugh in the midst of a serious apology.

"First, I want to apologize for being abrupt with you earlier in the woods. I was upset with my grandfather, and I took it out on you. On so many levels, he should have known better than to take you out in those woods without the proper gear or alerting anyone to where you were going. When I see him, I'm going to read him the riot act."

"No!" Grace cried out. "Please don't do that. Jasper didn't mean any harm. I wanted to see the cave, and I was the one who volunteered to go get help. If I wasn't so directionally challenged, things wouldn't have gotten so out of control."

Boone frowned at her. "Grace, you shouldn't be taking the blame for this."

"Why does there have to be blame? Can't we just chalk this up to an unfortunate incident?"

It was sweet of her to try to protect Jasper. Truthfully, that was normally his job. Protecting the ones he loved was an exhausting, often thankless endeavor. But he wouldn't have it any other way. Ever since his parents divorced and went their own ways—his mother had left Alaska for San Diego while his father had chosen to explore the world after nearly losing his life in an accident—he'd felt the gravity of being the head of the family.

Boone darted a quick glance at Grace. Although it was awkward, he needed to bring up the other matter. He cleared his throat and turned his gaze back to the road. "I also need to say I'm sorry for putting you in the midst of a family squabble. I hope it wasn't too uncomfortable."

He could feel the heat of Grace's gaze. "I would think it was a whole lot more uncomfortable for you, what with Honor putting your business out there."

"Honor thinks I sabotaged her plans to elope with her high school boyfriend based on my own…er, situation. That's far from the truth. As a law enforcement officer, I had no intention of allowing my baby sister to marry a petty thief. This guy had a rap sheet for breaking and entering, as well as underage drinking."

"So were they in love?"

Boone shrugged. "They were eighteen. Who even knows what love is it at that age?" He let out a sharp laugh. "I didn't know squat about love when I was their age."

"Hmm. I see," Grace said in a cryptic voice.

"What do you see?" Boone asked, feeling a little prickly. It was still a touchy subject for him since he hadn't yet been able to mend their relationship.

"I see why she's so upset with you. Not only did you get in the way of her plans, but you failed to acknowledge that she loved this man. That must have stung like crazy. To lose the man you love and to feel discounted by your older brother. Then to be sent away. That's a lot to swallow."

Boone shocked himself by not driving off the road into a ditch. Grace was siding with Honor? The way she made it sound, he came off looking like the bad guy. That was a first. More times than not he was hailed as a hero in town for saving Honor from disgrace and a teenage elopement. Not to mention how he'd paid for four years of college and a year of grad school.

Grace continued. "What I also see is that your sister is still immature, ungrateful and a tad on the rude side. She's also very sad. I could see it in her eyes."

Honor was sad? That gutted him. He felt partly, if not fully, responsible. Over the years he'd tried to justify his actions by telling himself that he'd rescued her from a life of ridicule and poverty and disgrace. But he'd never paused to ask if she was really and truly in love with Joshua.

He let out a ragged breath. "I hate to think of her that

way. Before…she was always Little Miss Sunshine. The brightest light in the room."

"I'm sorry about…well, you know. What Honor said about your girlfriend stepping out on you. Clearly, she spoke out of anger, but it was all kinds of wrong for her to bring that up."

Grace didn't know the half of it! He wasn't about to tell her the nitty-gritty details of Diana's grand deception or how it had affected him. It might fall under the category of "too much information." At the time it had felt as if his heart might shatter. He'd come to realize that his pride had been hurt more than anything. It was hard to hold your head up high as a law enforcement officer when the whole town knew you'd been played for a fool. Now at least he could discuss it without feeling as if a knife was lodged in his back.

"It's water under the bridge. Diana actually did me a favor. I'd been looking at engagement rings for a few months before I discovered she was running around with a high school buddy of mine. Finding out someone betrayed you and lied to you over and over again is difficult to process. It was painful, but it's better I found out before we walked down the aisle, right?"

He cast a glance at Grace. She resembled a deer caught in the headlights. For a woman who appeared to have an opinion about everything, she seemed at a loss for words. Rather than speak, she simply nodded her head. They settled into the silence, with Grace peering out the window as he navigated the snow-packed roads with all the finesse and care of a man who'd grown up in Alaska and knew the inherent dangers of the wintry weather.

"You don't owe me any apologies, Boone." Grace's voice cut into the silence. "You came to find me in the woods and took me to your brother's house for medical treatment. After all that he's lost and with everything he's going through, Liam didn't have to open up his home to me. But he did. That means a lot to me. What happened between you and Honor was real. Frankly, I wish my family was more like yours."

Grace's voice sounded so poignant, it stirred something deep inside him.

"Your family doesn't hash things out?"

"No," she said in a quiet voice. "They stuff everything down so they won't have to deal with it. But it only serves to create distance between us. We're like pieces of drift ice, all floating near each other without ever connecting."

Boone pulled into the Black Bear Cabins and put the car in park in front of Grace's cabin just as she voiced her truths about her family.

"I'm sorry about that," he said, turning toward her. "Connections with the people around us make our lives better... They make us stronger." In profile, her expression appeared contemplative. She didn't look in his direction. Instead she gazed down at her lap and fumbled with her bandaged fingers.

"It's no big deal," she muttered.

He reached out and lifted her chin up with his fingers. "Isn't it?" he asked, instantly realizing he was in way over his head now that he'd touched Grace. The feelings she evoked in him were akin to a punch in the gut. An electric current flowed between them. Her full, ruby lips parted as if she knew instinctively where this was going. He moved toward Grace so that their faces were within inches of each other. The urge to kiss her was undeniable. Just as he was about to lower his head to plant a kiss on

Grace's lips, the sound of someone screaming her name shattered the tranquillity of the moment.

Grace closed her eyes in anticipation of Boone's kiss. The truth was, she'd been wanting this kiss since the first time she laid eyes on him.

"Grace. I think Sophie is trying to get your attention." Boone's voice jolted her out of her reverie. *He wasn't kissing her. Why wasn't the sheriff of Love kissing her?*

Her eyes fluttered open. Instead of gazing in her direction, Boone was staring at something outside of the passenger side window. Then she heard it. "Grace! Grace!" Sophie's voice washed over her like a trombone.

She turned to look out her window. Sophie was standing there, snow falling all around her as she waved her arms in the air and screamed out her name. Grace let out a sigh. Sophie looked so endearing and sincere. Grace couldn't even be upset with her for busting up the romantic mood between her and Boone.

Grace turned back toward Boone. If she wasn't mistaken, he looked a little irritated. There were slight shadows under his eyes and a look of fatigue stamped on his face. It had been a long day for both of them.

"I guess we should call it a night," Boone drawled, his dark eyes glinting in the light from the cabins.

"Thanks for everything," she said, suddenly feeling shy in the aftermath of their almost kiss.

It had been an almost kiss, hadn't it? Unless of course she'd read the whole thing wrong. *Oh, no!* She'd closed her eyes and parted her lips. What must he think of her?

"Let me get the door for you." Boone stepped down from the truck and quickly made his way around to her door. Once he opened it, he took her hand as she stepped down.

"Oh, Grace. I've been so worried about you." Sophie reached out and wrapped her arms around her. Although she'd never considered herself a hugger, it was nice to be greeted so warmly by Sophie. After so many years of feeling like she didn't matter, she suddenly felt as if she did. This sensation might even trump the discomfort and fear she'd experienced being lost in the Nottingham Woods.

"Thanks for sending the cavalry to the rescue. If you hadn't raised the alarm, I'm not sure what might have happened." She shivered at the thought of it. It was nice, she realized, having connections with people who cared about your well-being. She'd never had a security blanket before.

Sophie beamed at her. "I've got your back. What are girlfriends for?"

"Ladies, you should get inside," Boone advised. "Grace shouldn't be exposed to frigid temperatures right now." After waving at Boone, Sophie tugged on Grace's arm and led her toward the porch.

All of a sudden Grace remembered something she'd forgotten to tell Boone. Something important. She turned around and called out to him. "Boone. Wait."

He stopped in his tracks as she walked over to him. His big brown eyes were full of curiosity. "You're a great big brother. Any girl would be blessed to have you." The words came out in a rush. "I just wanted to tell you that." Even though she believed he could have handled things better with Honor and her boyfriend, she admired the way he loved and protected his little sister. It was clear he had her best interest at heart. He needed to know that.

Boone nodded in acknowledgment. He grinned at her,

showcasing a pearly smile. "That means a lot. Thanks for telling me. Good night, Gracie."

With a self-conscious grin, she walked toward Sophie, who was standing on the porch with an all-knowing smile on her face.

Boone had called her Gracie. No one in her life had done that since her grandfather. Not ever! She wasn't a Gracie! Or was she? Ever since she'd arrived in Love, she hadn't felt like Grace Corbett of New York City. It was the oddest feeling. It was as if she'd reinvented herself the moment she arrived in Alaska. Gracie was kinder and gentler and more open to the world around her. She prayed to God and, even though she wasn't certain of it, she thought He might be listening.

So much had happened today. She felt as if a door had been pushed wide open. Now she knew what made Boone tick. His love for his family and his desire to protect them defined him. And much like herself, he'd been betrayed by the person he loved. She'd tried to summon the courage to tell him about her own heartbreak, but she hadn't wanted to see the look of pity in his eyes when she told him about Trey and being jilted at the altar. As humiliating as that had been, it was even worse that her own family had tossed her aside in the aftermath. It made her feel guilty knowing he'd laid it all out there for her while she'd kept quiet about her own past.

Finding out someone betrayed you and lied to you over and over again is difficult to process.

Boone's words were now seared into her consciousness. He'd been burned before by a woman who'd lied to him. And even though there was a world of difference between herself and Diana, she was operating in a really murky area. She was pretending to be something she wasn't.

It didn't feel great allowing Boone to believe she was in town as a participant in Operation Love. She wasn't in town to find love. Not even close. She was here to study the residents of this lovelorn town and to write a series of articles about her findings for the *Tribune*. That was her truth in black and white. There really weren't any shades of gray in this situation.

She hadn't expected to meet someone like Boone. He was heroic and strong, and he'd stepped in on several occasions to rescue her. There was a tenderness about him that he tried to hide. But she saw right through his rough edges. They'd almost shared their first kiss tonight. And even though she wanted to lock lips with Boone more than she wanted her next breath, she knew it would only lead her further astray from her goal. For the next six weeks she needed to keep her eyes on the prize and not on the handsome sheriff of Love!

Chapter Seven

"Why don't you just take a picture of Grace? It might last longer," Declan teased. His blue eyes were filled with amusement. Little crease lines surrounded his mouth and eyes as he teased Boone for watching Grace work in the Moose Café a couple days after her adventure.

"Don't you have a sightseeing tour lined up?" Boone asked, his eyes straying right back to Grace. She looked prettier than ever today, even though she was wearing a brown T-shirt with a moose on it. He shook his head and chuckled. Cameron and his corny Moose Café T-shirts!

Declan took a bite of his sandwich and washed it down with a glass of milk. "They canceled. Plus, it's way more fun to sit here and watch you get all goo-goo eyed over the new girl."

Boone gave Declan his most forbidding scowl. "I've never been goo-goo eyed in my life."

"There's a first time for everything," Declan said, his lips twitching with mirth. "I like this Grace Corbett. She mellows you out."

Boone shifted his gaze back toward Grace. He watched as she gracefully placed one hand on her hip. She had a pot of coffee in the other. Boone knew he should be listening to Gunther and Abel as they read their love letters aloud to him and Declan. He'd agreed to give them his opinion. No matter how hard he tried, he couldn't seem to take his eyes off Grace as she moved from table to table refilling coffee cups. Perhaps he was getting his fill now since she hadn't been at work yesterday. Cameron, feeling guilty that he hadn't stepped in and stopped Jasper from being Grace's tour guide, had given her the day off work to rest. It was a good thing, too, since she still had a few bandages on her fingers.

He'd been forced to face the cold hard truth yesterday when he'd arrived at the Moose Café and realized he wouldn't be seeing Grace. The ache inside him had been acute. He'd felt deprived of her company. His thoughts had drifted in her direction all day long. He'd never admit it to his best friend in a million years, but he was right. He was goo-goo eyed over Grace Corbett. For so long he'd prayed for the Lord to send him a woman who could move his heart. Never in a million years had he expected God to send him a woman like Grace.

She was a beautiful city girl who seemed to be a mass of contradictions. Girly, but as tough as nails. Sweet, but sassy. Smart, yet impractical when it came to wearing high-heeled shoes in Alaska. Friendly, yet a bit guarded.

As Grace moved toward their table, her eyes locked with his. He felt a warmth spreading across his chest. An awareness flared between them. Not for the first time, he kicked himself for not planting a kiss on Grace's lips the other night. The past two nights he'd lain awake thinking about it. He'd imagined how it would feel to kiss her, and if it was something Grace wanted as badly as he did. If he was reading the signals right, she felt something for him. Something he wanted to explore.

"Roses are red, violets are blue. I can't wait to spend some more time with you." Gunther beamed as he finished reading his letter and placed it down on the table. "What do you think? I'm going to give it to her right before the ice-skating social."

Abel shook his head vigorously. "It's real solid. She'll love it."

Lionel pulled up a chair, sat himself down and gave Gunther a thumbs-up.

"I think she'll be mighty pleased with that prose," Boone said.

"Sounds like something I got in second grade on Valentine's Day," Declan muttered as Boone lightly kicked him under the table.

Grace reached for a coffee cup and began to fill it up. "Gunther. You're hoping to land the girl of your dreams. Am I right?"

"Yes, Grace. Wanda is my everything. She thinks I need to be more romantic, so I want to show her that I can rise to the challenge."

She pointed her finger at Gunther's poem. "No offense, but that right there is not going to seal the deal."

Gunther frowned. "No?" His shoulders sagged. "What's wrong with it?"

Grace shook her head and looked around the table at each of them. "You men just don't get it, do you? Letters are incredibly romantic." She sighed "There's nothing like receiving a nice, crisp envelope in the mail and being able to sit back and lose yourself in someone's flowery sentiments about you. Women want to be romanced. Wooed. Courted. We want someone to make us feel as if we're the earth, moon, sun and the stars."

"That's the way I feel about Wanda," Gunther said. "I've waited my whole life for someone like her."

Grace bestowed a stunning smile on Gunther. "Then tell her. Use your words and show her how she makes you feel. Here." She placed her hand over her heart. "I'm a pretty good letter writer if you need some help."

"Would you?" Gunther leaned forward in his chair, his expression radiating excitement.

"Of course I will. I'll have to wait for my break, though. The boss can be a bit of a grouch," she said in a stage whisper. Boone wanted to laugh out loud at the comical expression on her face.

"I could use some help, too," Lionel piped up. "Don't leave me hanging. I'd love to do something to get Anabel's attention."

"Oh, Lionel. I'd never leave you in the lurch," Grace said, reaching out and touching Lionel's arm. "I'd love to hear all about your courtship. How you met, what made you think she was the one, where you see things going."

Boone didn't like the feeling of possessiveness sweeping over him. It annoyed him to no end. He shouldn't have the sudden urge to knock his friend's chair over, should he? Why should his gut tighten at the sight of Grace sitting next to Lionel, Abel and Gunther as she helped them with their love letters?

He tried to look away, but he found his eyes glued to the graceful curve of her neck and her onyx locks. A woman like Grace was all wrong for him. He imagined that a city girl like Grace would expect a man to buy her expensive shoes or take her on shopping sprees. He was a simple man with a very ordered, uncomplicated life.

Any woman who thought she could lead him around by the nose was in for the surprise of her life.

So why did the mere sight of Grace cause his belly to clench up? And why was he filled with so much regret about not kissing her the other night?

The one thing he didn't regret were the emotions roaring through him. It had been ages since he'd experienced anything remotely like this. And it made him feel more present and more alive than he'd felt in years. As much as he loved his siblings, he'd sacrificed his own personal life under the weight of all their issues. Although he didn't regret a moment spent caring for them, he often wondered if he'd deliberately focused on their lives rather than on his own. Had it been his way of staying out of the danger zone?

On his way back to his office, he strolled by the counter where Grace was sitting down enjoying a coffee and a cinnamon bun.

"Awful nice of you to take the time to help out with the letters. Once word gets out, you're going to have a line going out the door."

Grace appeared to be brushing crumbs off the sides of her mouth. "I enjoy helping them. I just hope they don't get their hopes up too high."

"What do you mean?" Boone asked. "Isn't hope a good thing?"

"They seem so...invested in these women. They've really poured their heart and souls into these letters." Grace's eyes radiated concern.

Boone raised an eyebrow. "Shouldn't they be invested? They're courting them with the hopes of marrying 'em. I'd call that an investment."

"Even more reason that they should be careful," Grace

said as she tied her apron back on and headed behind the counter to finish her shift.

Grace's cryptic comment left him scratching his head. Had life taught Grace to be leery of happily-ever-after? And if so, what experiences had led her to feel so strongly about the subject? Now that he thought about it, he realized it was high time he learned more about Grace Corbett.

Boone had been dead-on about the demand for her writing services. Over the next few days, one by one, men trickled in to the Moose Café asking for her assistance. They were incredibly sincere and determined to find the right words to court their ladies. Seeing so many men go the extra distance to woo their women was impressive. She helped as many as she could before Cameron pulled her aside and sternly reminded her she was on the clock.

On the clock. Yet another reminder that time was ticking away from her.

A phone call this morning from Tony had reminded her that she needed to focus her energies on her assignment rather than good-looking lawmen and sweet-faced, whiskered mayors. When she'd seen the New York City area code on her caller ID, something inside her had wanted to ignore that call. It was surprising, since she'd jumped through hoops for the past four years to impress her boss. Shouldn't personal attention from Tony be a validation of everything she'd worked so hard to achieve?

"Grace! How are you? It's Tony." His thick, New York accent rang out over the line.

"I'm doing well, Tony. So far, so good."

"Just calling to check in. I was expecting some sort

of update from you by now. Perhaps a sneak peek of the first article."

A feeling of annoyance flooded her. *An update?* She'd been in Love for less than a week. Leave it to her boss to expect everything to happen at warp speed.

"I've been laying the groundwork for the series. There's no need to worry. It's going to be great. I've been meeting lots of interesting people and finding out the secret history of the town. I'm going to a tea to meet some of the ladies who moved here for Operation Love."

A long silence ensued.

"Tony? Are you still there?"

"I don't have to remind you of how much is riding on this series. With faltering sales and consumers flocking to the internet for their news, the newspaper business is at a crossroads. We've put considerable resources behind you, Grace. This series has to be a blockbuster."

Grace swallowed past the lump in her throat. *Block-buster? Sure! No pressure.*

"Oh, it will be, Tony. There's a veritable gold mine of information here." *Gold mine. No pun intended.*

"Keep your eye on the prize, Grace."

By the time the call had ended, she felt a sense of urgency about her assignment. Tony had sounded fairly grim over the phone. There was a lot of behind-the-scenes politics involved with running a newspaper. She could only imagine what pressures he was facing, but now it was trickling down to her. Fear nestled its way inside her. She couldn't lose her job! It was the one constant in her life. When her world had turned upside down two years ago, she'd buried herself up to her elbows in her work. It had been a lifeline. It served as proof that she wasn't a total failure.

Later this afternoon Hazel was hosting a "welcome to Love" tea for all the new women in town. The social event would give her an opportunity to find out more about the participants in Operation Love. There were so many burning questions she needed to ask. What had motivated them to come all the way to Alaska to find love? Were they serious about marrying one of the men? Did they imagine themselves settling down here?

Now that she'd met and befriended Gunther, Lionel and Abel, she felt invested in the outcome of their romances. There was no way in the world she was going to sit by idly and watch anyone take advantage of their sweet natures and their eagerness to find love. She'd been on the receiving end of heartbreak, and she knew firsthand how it devastated a person's life. Especially when it came out of the blue. She didn't want the same thing to happen to them. If these ladies didn't pass muster, she was prepared to do anything in her power to dismantle the relationships.

Before Grace knew it, several hours had flown by, and she and Sophie were making their way to the lodge to help Hazel prepare for the tea party. She couldn't help but smile as she looked around at all the beautiful, decorative accents scattered around the room. The overall effect was lovely.

"Thanks for helping out, girls. What I know about tea parties would fit on a postage stamp," Hazel said with a grateful smile.

"I think this is just about the prettiest table set for high tea that I've ever seen," Sophie declared.

"I've had this china for thirty years. It was supposed to be part of my trousseau, but I never did get married."

Hazel's voice held a note of wistfulness that was hard to ignore. "That ship sailed."

"You never know, Hazel," Grace said. "Love doesn't have an expiration date."

Stop the presses! Those words hadn't really just come flying out of her mouth, had they? She was beginning to sound like a sappy greeting card.

"Grace is right, Hazel. Love may be right around the corner," Sophie said in a chipper tone.

"From your lips to God's ears," Hazel said as she tilted her head and looked upward. Both Sophie and Grace laughed at the expectant expression on Hazel's face. Grace had a sneaking suspicion that Hazel's feelings for Jasper were not platonic, but she would never ask her outright. She prayed Hazel would find a love to sustain her through the good times and the bad.

"Oh, I almost forgot," Grace said as she reached for the floral bouquet. She placed the vase containing baby's breath and forget-me-nots, the official state flower of Alaska, in the middle of the table. She stood back and looked at the table with a critical eye. Everything looked perfect.

Ten ladies in all would be coming today. Six of them had found matches in town already. She'd already peppered Hazel with questions about which of the ladies was actively in a relationship, so she had a good idea of which women she should pump for information during the tea. Helping out Hazel was so much fun, she'd almost forgotten that it wouldn't be a purely social event. For her, it would be a means to an end.

The women began arriving two and three at a time. There was such a range in ages, heights, sizes and skin colors. Seeing such a diverse group made Grace smile.

It reminded her of being back home and walking around New York City where she saw a melting pot of people on a daily basis.

Grace looked down at her outfit. She'd dressed up for the tea party in a cute black-and-cream dress with three-quarter length sleeves. Once she'd reached the lodge, her boots had been replaced by a pretty pair of red heels. Most of the women were dressed in slacks and sweaters. Almost all of them had arrived wearing Hazel's boots, which they'd since taken off and replaced with flats. If Hazel ever decided to get serious about selling her boots, the women in this room could be a great marketing tool.

Her ears immediately perked up when a woman stuck out her hand and introduced herself as Wanda. Gunther's girlfriend was a tall, big-boned woman with dirty-blond hair and an easy smile. One by one the women came into the lodge. Anabel. Lucy. Claire. After a while, Grace couldn't remember all their names anymore. But it was nice to be in the midst of so many women. So far, she hadn't seen all that many in town or at the Moose Café. There really was a serious woman shortage here in Love.

There was a buzz of activity in the room that reminded Grace of a hive of bees. Everyone seemed happy to be at the lodge, mingling and enjoying cucumber sandwiches, pastries, blueberry tarts and an assortment of teas. The atmosphere was upbeat and friendly. All the ladies seemed completely at ease.

Hazel, wearing a floral skirt that hung well past her knees, clapped her hands together to get everyone's attention. "Thanks for coming, ladies. Everyone take a seat." Hazel motioned toward the elegantly laid table in the dining room. Once everyone had taken their place at the table, she continued. "The main reason for us gathering here today is to officially welcome you to Love and to be able to meet in fellowship as women who are living the Alaskan lifestyle. It's important when you live in a community like Love to establish the bonds of friendship and solidarity. It can be an isolating experience due to the weather and the lack of sunlight. That's one of the reasons we're having the ice-skating social on Saturday." She let out a hearty chuckle. "I know from firsthand experience how intimidating it can be to acclimate to Alaska. The driving conditions. The frigid temperatures. Trying to make sense out of reindeer sausage." A collective laugh rose up among the group. Grace noticed a few women making faces at the mention of reindeer as a food source.

"I asked Pastor Jack to stop by to offer his support and prayers. If you haven't met him yet, he's the good-looking guy in the room. The only guy I might add," Hazel said with a laugh.

Grace had never seen a pastor like the one who'd arrived a few moments ago. He was young—way younger than the pastor at her family's church. Early thirties, she would guess. He was a handsome man with cocoa-brown skin and a smile that wouldn't quit. He was wearing fashionable jeans and a chunky wool sweater. Everyone welcomed him with enthusiasm and huge grins.

He looked around the table, a beautiful smile etched on his face. "Let's hold hands everyone. It's a simple way of connecting with one another. We're all pieces of the same puzzle, after all." Everyone reached out and held hands around the table as Pastor Jack began to recite his blessing. "Dear Lord, we ask that You bless this wonderful group of women on their journey. They've come here as an act of faith and in order to live in love, the way You intended. Lord, please safeguard and protect them during the rough moments that may crop up on the road ahead. Hold each of them in the palm of Your hand and point her toward everlasting love."

A hush fell over the table as Pastor Jack's words seeped into the atmosphere. In all her life, Grace had never listened to a prayer as poignant as the one she'd just heard. It humbled her to be included in such a rich and moving prayer. When was the last time anyone had prayed for her? Again, she felt a sliver of discomfort at the knowledge that she wasn't in the same category as these other women. She didn't deserve to be included in Pastor Jack's prayers.

Later, as the social wound down, Grace found herself reluctant to say goodbye to all her new friends. She made a point to invite them to stop in to the Moose Café for a complimentary cappuccino, per Cameron's instructions. Although she knew he regarded it as a business promotion, she'd be thrilled to reconnect with these women and see them on a regular basis.

"Grace." She turned around to find Wanda looking at her with a contented smile. "I just wanted to say thank you. I know you helped Gunther put all those beautiful words down on paper."

She shook her head. "Those were his sentiments. I just helped him shape them a little bit. He deserves all the credit."

"Well, he sure speaks highly of you. He said you were incredibly generous with your time."

She felt her cheeks flushing with all the praise Wanda was heaping on her. "It was my pleasure," Grace said. "He's a wonderful guy."

"He is," Wanda gushed. "I feel so blessed to have met him right off the bat. When I first arrived here in Love,

I wondered whether or not I'd made a mistake in coming here. Everyone in my family told me I was all kinds of crazy to pack up and leave Oregon for Alaska. But I really feel that God pointed me in this direction after I read Mayor Prescott's article." She lowered her voice to a whisper. "This may sound strange, but I felt as if Jasper was talking directly to me."

"Jasper does have that effect on people," Grace answered. Thoughts of Jasper usually caused her to smile. The morning after their adventure in Nottingham Woods she'd received a beautiful floral arrangement at her cabin, courtesy of the mayor. The attached note had read, *"So happy to hear you're doing well. Thanks for being such a trouper. So thrilled you decided to live in Love."*

"He's pretty special," Grace conceded. For the first time she realized that Jasper reminded her of her own grandfather. They both had spunk, determination and an innate ability to connect with people. Grace felt the sharp ache of loss she always experienced when she remembered Grandpa Corbett. Certain holes were never filled.

"All of us owe him a debt of gratitude," Wanda said in a raised voice. "Without Operation Love I'd still be back in Oregon working at the family produce farm."

"So, do you think you've met the one?" Grace asked. Wanda seemed very sweet, but if she was wishy-washy about Gunther, the poor man needed to know not to put all his eggs in one basket. After all, most of the females would have their pick of any man in town given the imbalance.

Wanda tucked her head down. Her cheeks turned rosy. When she lifted her head up there was a sheen of moisture in her eyes. "Yes, I do. I know life isn't always going to be easy living here in Love, but I'd be honored to live out the rest of my days with Gunther."

And there it was. Wanda was head over heels in love with Gunther. It oozed out of every pore in her body. It glistened in her eyes. Her voice overflowed with sincerity. Her feelings were the real deal. Grace was ashamed for doubting her and assuming the worst.

A feeling of relief flooded through her at the knowledge that there might be a happy ending for Gunther and Wanda. "I'm happy for the two of you. You're very blessed."

"Don't worry, Grace," Wanda said. "You'll meet someone soon. Unless of course you already have," she said with a wink.

Boone's handsome face came to mind. The sandybrown hair that sometimes fell across his forehead and almost hid his eyes. The eyes that always seemed to see straight through her, right down to the things that mattered most of all. The laughter that emanated from deep inside him and wrapped itself around her like a cloak.

She had met someone. The type of someone who made it impossible for her to even glance in another man's direction. Whenever he was nearby, she had the sensation of needing to catch her breath. He was funny and protective. He'd rescued her on three separate occasions. Although she was an independent city girl, he made her feel safe and sound. She let out a sigh as she struggled to process what was happening to her. Falling for Sheriff Boone Prescott wasn't on her to-do list. Her life in New York City meant the world to her. She couldn't imagine giving up her life there or her job at the *Tribune*.

Grace glanced around the room. Everyone in attendance had pure motives for disrupting their lives and ven-

turing so far off the grid. She'd talked to most of them and
overheard snippets of their conversations. They wanted
love. True, enduring love. They'd all collectively decided
to put together an ice-skating social so they could all
become part of the Love community. Despite her cyni-
cism, all the women seemed authentic and down-to-earth.
There didn't appear to be a bad one in the bunch. So far
she was the only one who was in town under false pretenses. And although she had wanted to relax and fully
enjoy the camaraderie and festivities related to the tea
party, there was a part of her that couldn't let down her
guard. She only had five weeks left in Love, and there
was no point in making friends with these women. Even
though she was starting to fall in love with this charming Alaskan village, she couldn't pretend that her future
resided here. There wouldn't be any happy ending for
her and Boone. If he discovered her true agenda in Love,
there was no doubt in her mind that he would want nothing to do with her.

As he walked into the Moose Café, Boone felt a surge
of disappointment upon remembering that today was the
tea party at the Black Bear Lodge. Grace would be miss-
ing in action. He felt a little ashamed of himself for having considered searching for information about Grace
online last evening. With dozens of Grace Corbetts possibly residing in New York State, he imagined it would
have been an exercise in futility. He felt foolish for even
considering such a thing, even though he was curious
about her background. Up to this point she'd done nothing to warrant his suspicions other than pad her résumé
and wear inappropriate shoes. Yep. It was official. He
was losing his mind over Grace.

At least a hearty meal would be a diversion from his recurring thoughts of her. Cameron had called him earlier and invited him for lunch. Boone was torn between being optimistic about the status of their relationship and suspicious of Cameron's motives. Once they sat down to a lunch of caribou stew and sandwiches, Cameron brought up what was on his mind.

"So, Honor's back, huh? Guess I'm the last to know."

Boone put his sandwich back down on his plate. "You didn't know? I assumed I was the last to know."

"I didn't know a thing until she called me this morning." Cameron paused. He wrinkled his nose. "She was asking about Joshua."

Joshua? Five years later and Honor still had her high school boyfriend at the forefront of her mind. He let out a tremendous sigh. "Did you tell her?"

Cameron nodded. "Yeah. I figured it was best coming from me rather than her finding out some other way."

"Did she seem…upset?"

Cameron leveled Boone with a stone-cold glare. "What do you think?"

"I think finding out he married someone else might give her closure." He took another bite of his sandwich as thoughts of the past swirled around in his head.

"Well, if you consider crying your eyes out as closure, then our baby sister got it in droves today."

Boone winced at the idea of Honor being in such distress over a man who wasn't worth her time or devotion. If he could absorb some of her pain, he'd willingly do so. Since she'd been gone from Love, Joshua had been in all sorts of trouble. Boone had arrested him three times for various infractions, the most memorable of which was being drunk and disorderly on a snowmobile as naked as the day he was born. Last year he'd left Love and gotten married to someone in the Lower 48. Unlike Honor, he'd moved on. What would it take for his sister to stop romanticizing her first love?

Cameron sat back in his chair and folded his arms across his chest. He locked gazes with Boone. "By the way, I know you haven't been hanging around here for the turkey and brie sandwiches."

Boone tried to look unassuming. "No? They're mighty tasty if you're looking for some customer feedback. Just between you and me, a tomato might raise it to the level of sheer perfection."

Cameron rolled his eyes. "In case you're interested, I heard some guys talking about asking Grace to the skating social. Hank's been coming in here two, three times a day to catch a glimpse of her. You might want to bite the bullet and ask her first, if you're so inclined."

Hank Jeffries! He was a fireman and an all-around good guy. There wasn't a single negative thing Boone could say about him. The idea of Hank courting Grace caused an unsettled feeling to roll around in the pit of his stomach. It made him wonder if Grace might not fall for a guy like Hank.

"I don't know," he hedged. "It's been a while since I've put my foot in the dating pond."

Cameron narrowed his eyes at him. "You like her. Just admit it."

Boone nodded, feeling as though he was back in grade school when he and his brothers would talk about the girls they were sweet on.

"I like her. A lot," he acknowledged. Just saying the words out loud scared him a little. And it was too late to take them back. He'd put it out there in the universe.

It made everything brewing between him and Grace all too real.

"She likes you, too, from what I can tell," Cameron said. "You can see the chemistry between the two of you from a mile away."

It reassured him to hear Cameron's opinion on the matter. The strain between them was beginning to ease up some. He was getting his little brother back, one day at a time. He just needed to be patient and let their relationship get back on track. The truth was he felt a little rusty about all the rules of dating and the signs of a woman's interest. It had been a very long time since he'd had more than a passing interest in getting to know someone. What he felt for Grace was beginning to feel like the real thing. It was making him question what he wanted in the future.

"And you? Any interest in making a love connection?" He tossed the question out to Cameron with all the ease of a professional pitcher.

Cameron's facial features tensed up. "I don't want to talk about me. There's no one I'm interested in romantically, and that's a fact." Cameron's tone was brusque, and it brooked no argument.

In that moment he saw everything his brother wasn't saying. "You still love her, don't you?" he asked, the words rushing out of his mouth before he could stem the tide.

"You just can't leave well enough alone, can you?" With a movement that almost overturned his chair, Cameron jumped up, grabbed both their bowls and stomped off toward the kitchen. Boone felt as if he'd taken six steps backward in his relationship with Cameron when he heard the crash of dishes being thrown in the sink.

As far as love was concerned, he and Cameron had one thing in common. They'd both been betrayed by the woman they'd loved. But he no longer loved Diana. And he'd come to realize that their relationship had been about as deep as the water in a kiddie pool. Cameron, on the other hand, still loved Paige, a woman who had conspired with her own father to fleece the town of Love and had made his brother an object of ridicule. All things considered, he felt mighty fortunate.

Chapter Eight

Grace's fingers flew over the keyboard as she wrote about her spelunking adventures with Jasper. It was her day off from the Moose Café, and she was determined to finish her first article based on her initial impressions of Love. Reading back her words caused prickles of awareness to pop up on her arm. A feeling of excitement raced through her. It always felt like this when a story started to come together. Once she returned home to New York City, the first of the articles would be released. One by one they would trickle out. And then the truth would be revealed. Grace shut her eyes tightly as Boone's face came into sharp focus. What would he think of her? It hurt her to even imagine how it would all play out.

Maybe, just maybe, they wouldn't find out. This particular village was somewhat removed from what was happening in the rest of the country. *Who was she kidding?* There was cable news here, as well as internet access. Everyone here in Love would know she'd come to town with an agenda that didn't include falling in love. As it was, Hazel kept grilling her about which man in town she had her eye on. More times than not, she asked her about Boone, telling her that if she was twenty years younger, she'd chase after him herself. Bless Hazel. She always made her laugh. She was going to miss her like crazy when it was time to leave Love.

Grace stopped typing and looked out her window at the last vestiges of sunlight. In a few minutes the sun would be stamped out from the sky, and the night would prematurely come into being. According to Boone, every day they inched closer to winter they lost a little bit of sunlight. Pretty soon, there would only be four to five hours a day of sunlight. It would be kind of cool to experience it.

But you won't be here then, she reminded herself. *You'll be long gone.*

The thought of no longer being in Love left her feeling as if someone had placed a heavy weight on her chest. More and more she could imagine herself living here, and it wounded her to think about leaving this memorable town. She shook the raw emotion away, chiding herself for being so sentimental. This wasn't her home. It was a job assignment!

The sound of tires crunching outside on the snow had her standing up to get a clear view of the driveway. Boone's blue-and-white cruiser came to a stop in front of her cabin. Excitement unfurled inside her at the prospect of seeing him on a day she hadn't expected to even venture outside. She walked over to the desk and shut her computer before tucking her notes inside the drawer.

Before he could knock, she flung the door open, her heart constricting at the sight of him. He was dressed in his uniform, and he held his hat in his hand, pressed tightly against his chest. Sturdy boots encased his feet.

"Afternoon, Grace," he said with a nod.

"Afternoon. What brings you out here, Boone? Helping Hazel track down Primrose again?" she teased. Every time she thought of the night Boone had introduced her to Hazel's skunk, it made her smile.

His lips began to twitch, right before he flashed a wide, easygoing grin. "Not this time. Actually I wanted to talk to you, if you have a few minutes."

"Come on in. I was just about to make some hot chocolate." Her curiosity was instantly piqued by whatever had motivated Boone to pay her a visit this afternoon.

"I'd like to take you to the skating social." The words gushed out of Boone's mouth like a rushing river.

Grace looked up at him as a feeling of surprise swept over her.

"As your date?" she asked.

Boone's face held a perplexed expression. "Yes. As my date."

"Then you should say that. 'Grace, I'd like you to be my date for the skating social.'"

He let out a little noise that resembled a groan. "Isn't that pretty much what I said?"

Grace shook her head. "No. You used the word *take*, not date. There's a world of difference."

Boone shoved his hand through his hair and shifted his stance. "Grace, would you like to—" he began.

"I'd love to," she said smoothly, bursting into giggles at the dumbfounded expression on Boone's face.

A slow hiss escaped Boone's lips. "I'll take that hot chocolate now if you're done toying with me."

She quickly ushered him inside her cabin. Once Boone entered her abode, it felt as if he overshadowed everything else with his height and breadth. The atmosphere instantly changed, making it feel all the more intimate.

"Take a seat while I put the kettle on," Grace said, tickled at the idea of Boone coming to see her on her day off in order to ask her out.

"Actually, no. Scratch that idea for the moment. Put your boots and jacket on, Gracie. I want to show you something."

She wrapped her arms around herself. "Right now? But it's so warm and cozy inside," she said, not relishing the idea of being outside in the frosty conditions.

"Come on. Take a walk on the wild side. It's twenty-four degrees outside. That's practically balmy." Boone was pleading with her with his eyes.

"Okay," she grumbled. "But this better be good. My major goal for today was to get out of bed and get dressed. My feet are killing me from standing on them all day yesterday."

Boone's lips twitched. "Imagine how much they'd be hurting if you'd continued to wear those four-inch heels."

Grace shuddered as she put her boots on. She let out a sigh of appreciation. The boots were a welcome relief for aching feet.

She still loved her high-heeled shoes, but the thought of standing around in them all day was not appealing. "I never thanked you for suggesting Hazel's boots. They've worked out beautifully."

She slid her arms through her coat sleeves, and Boone leaned in and zipped her coat up for her. "No, thanks needed. As I'm sure you know, Hazel gets a real kick out of seeing her boots walking around town. She almost had me wearing a pair." He winked at her. "Almost."

"She needs to start charging customers for the boots instead of bartering them for goods. Something tells me they're worth more than a dozen eggs and a pair of wool gloves. I had to practically force her to take payment from me," Grace grumbled.

Boone shrugged. "You make a good point. Unfortunately, Hazel doesn't look at the big picture. Perhaps you could give her a nudge in the right direction."

Grace liked that idea. If her fashion instincts were right, Hazel could make a small fortune off these boots!

Grace jammed a wool hat on and pulled it down past her ears. Once her mittens were on, she yanked open the door and stepped outside. The glare from the sun blinded her for a moment. Boone walked behind her down the steps and then stepped in front of her to lead the way.

Grace turned toward him. "Where are we going?"

Boone pointed down the long driveway toward the lodge. "Have you ever been down the Black Bear Trail?"

"Nope. The only trail I've been down is the one in Nottingham Woods. And we all know how that turned out," Grace joked.

"You were a real trouper in that situation." He stopped in his tracks and turned toward her. His expression was somber. "Just promise me you won't go off legend hunting with Jasper again. I know he can be really persistent about it. He's at a point in his life when he can't afford to have any more broken bones, and he's not rational when it comes to the legend. That ankle of his was pretty badly injured."

Grace felt a twinge of guilt about Jasper's ankle. She hadn't even known it was a break and not a sprain. Perhaps she should have nipped things in the bud before they'd even ventured into the woods. On the other hand, Jasper seemed to get such joy from his adventures. Surely that wasn't a bad thing.

She bit her lip. "All right, Boone. I promise not to entertain any more of Jasper's treasure-hunting ideas. The last thing I want is to see him get hurt."

Boone's expression relaxed. "Thank you. I know I may sound like I'm overreacting, but Jasper tends to take things way too far and he's had a few health issues this past year."

Grace shrugged. "You love him and you want to see him safe from harm. You don't have to apologize for that. Not to me or to anyone."

Boone nodded in her direction before continuing to walk down the road. She joined in, staying close beside him.

A few feet past the lodge, Boone pointed toward a wooden sign with white lettering standing next to an opening in a copse of pine trees. *Black Bear Trail.* Boone took the lead and charged ahead, his steps full of purpose. He waited for her to catch up and then walked side by side with her, stopping on occasion to point out a black-billed magpie or a raven. He showed her the difference between the types of trees they passed—Sitka spruce and western hemlock—and pointed in the direction of a black-tailed deer as it scampered off into the woods.

Wherever Grace looked, beauty surrounded her. It was different from anything she'd known before or had ever paused to appreciate. She couldn't think of a time back home when she'd stopped to simply appreciate her environment. She'd always justified it by telling herself that the busy schedule of a journalist didn't allow for such luxuries.

After about five minutes of walking along the trail, Boone stopped at the edge of a clearing and pointed at a cliff about thirty feet away. "Take a look."

She peered up at the side of the cliff, uncertain as to what was so special about it. "What am I looking at?"

"You'll see," Boone said in a lilting voice that hinted of something wonderful to come.

All of a sudden Grace spotted a bald eagle soaring across the sky. Within seconds, another joined the first one in flight. One after another, eagles majestically flew through the air. They were serene and beautiful. Their movements were powerful and full of grace. She'd never seen one in person, and since they'd been near extinction a few years ago, she'd feared that she might never have the opportunity.

"I can't believe there are so many of them," Grace said, her eyes darting all over the sky to catch a glimpse of them.

"We call it Eagle's Landing," Boone explained. "For some reason the eagles make their home way up there in a little alcove on the side of the cliff."

"It's their little nest," she said, her voice infused with awe. There hadn't been many times in her life when she'd felt speechless, but right here in this moment the raw beauty of the eagles stunned her into silence.

"Pretty amazing, huh?" Boone asked, his eyes roaming over her face.

She nodded her head, not trusting herself to speak and ruin the grandeur of the moment. She felt a sudden desire to write about all the things she was discovering about everyday life in Love. The wonderful people. The Moose Café. Wild eagles in flight. Hazel's comfy boots. Sheriffs who made house calls. There was so much more to this town than a woman shortage and Operation Love. There was pluck and determination and Alaskan pride. There was friendship and heart and fellowship. And she was beginning to think that complete and utter happiness might be here, just within reach.

Boone rubbed his hands together. "The temperature's beginning to drop out here. It might be time to head back. Hope that offer of hot chocolate still stands."

She smiled at Boone, knowing there was nothing she'd like better than to sit down with him over a mug of hot chocolate. Little by little her world was changing. Two weeks ago her happiness had centered around her job at the *Tribune*, adding to her massive shoe collection and planning her next beach getaway. A burst of contentment flooded her at the simplicity of her current wants. Being with Boone, taking a nature walk and the prospect of drinking hot chocolate gave her more joy than she'd ever dreamed possible. But would she be willing to uproot her life in New York City and all the things that went along with it? Would she be content to live a small-town rugged life? What about museums and twenty-four hour diners and towering buildings? How could she leave all that?

"Of course the offer still stands," she answered, feeling a slight panic at the realization that she was living on borrowed time. All too soon these moments would be nothing more than memories she reflected on from her tiny office in Manhattan. She needed to hold on tightly to these moments before they vanished in a puff of smoke.

It seemed to Boone as if the entire population of Love had shown up for the ice-skating event at Deer Run Lake. The welcoming committee had set up a snack table with hot chocolate, white-chocolate-chip cookies, hot apple cider and apple cider doughnuts. By the time they'd arrived, a good number of people were already on the ice, most of them kids who were whizzing around fast enough to make him dizzy.

When he noticed Grace shivering, he purchased two doughnuts and hot chocolates for the two of them. Eyes widened. Eyebrows rose. A few men frowned at him. By tomorrow morning he predicted that his date with Grace would be the talk of the town.

Did you see Sheriff Prescott last night?

I thought he'd never get over Diana.

Oddly, the thought of people gossiping about him didn't bother him as much as usual. Perhaps that had something to do with Grace being by his side. In her black ski jacket, dark leggings and pink tutu, she looked very fashion forward. Pink leg warmers topped it all off. She held a black bag in her hand that contained her skates. Now came the moment when he would have to break it to her.

"Ready to get out there?" Grace asked, a look of anticipation lighting up her face.

Boone quirked his mouth. "I don't know how to skate."

Grace shook her head. "That can't be true."

Boone held up his hand. "I promise you, it's true."

"But you live in Alaska, home of snow, ice and sub-zero temperatures. How did you make it through your childhood without knowing how to skate?" Grace's eyebrows rose by what seemed like inches.

"The Prescotts are fishermen, going back as far as we can trace it. I learned how to fish and mountain climb. And there was white-water rafting, skiing and canoeing. We Prescotts kept busy. We just weren't skating."

"Sounds like you Prescotts are a rugged bunch."

"That's a fair statement. Pretty much explains why my grandfather is still spelunking in his seventies. Look at you, though," Boone said as Grace unzipped her bag and pulled out a pair of beautiful white skates. "I'm impressed. You brought your skates and everything."

Grace's eyes sparkled as she lightly ran her hand over her skates. "I learned to skate when I was six. I used to love when my grandfather would take me skating at Central Park back home." Grace's eyes sparkled. "The cold wind whipping against my face, that feeling of flying as I soared across the ice, a mug of hot chocolate between my mittens as I warmed up afterward. It was as close to perfect as it got. Afterward he would take me to my favorite doll shop and let me pick out whichever one I wanted."

This was how Grace loved, he realized. Tenderly. Poignantly. With gusto. She shone from the inside out. What would it be like to be loved by this woman? To be her everything? To make it all the way past the wall she had up?

"Those are beautiful memories. Sounds like he's an important part of your life."

Grace winced. "He was. We lost him five years ago to a heart attack. Not a day goes by that I don't miss him."

Perhaps that was the reason she seemed to have taken such a liking to Jasper. It was possible that being around him reminded her of the grandfather she'd lost.

"So, I'm more than happy to teach you to skate." Grace said.

Boone looked over at the lake. "I don't think that would be a very good idea."

She put her hands on her hips. "And why not? You asked me out on a date, Boone Prescott, which means you have to see to it that I have a good time."

"And you can't have a good time unless I'm stumbling around on the ice?" Boone could picture it vividly in his mind's eye. At close to six foot two, he'd go down like a mighty spruce tree. It wouldn't be pretty. And then Grace would never want to go out with him again.

"I'll have a much better time if we're together out on the ice," she said sweetly, flashing him her most endearing smile. Grace's smile did a number on him. For the first time in his life he wished he could skate as proficiently as a professional hockey player, if only to whirl Grace around the ice and give her the date she'd imagined.

Boone shifted from one foot to the other. "If I had some skates I'd give it a try, but I don't own a pair."

Grace's lips twitched as if she was sitting on a secret. "Declan told me you might say that." *Declan? When had Grace spoken with Declan?*

All of a sudden Grace let out a loud whistle and gestured toward the ice. Declan, racing around the ice as if he was born with skates on, glided toward them. In a graceful motion he stopped short and walked off the ice straight toward them.

"Hi, Grace. Boone. I was waiting for you to arrive. My other pair of skates is in the bag over there by the tree." He nodded in the direction of a pine tree ten feet away. Declan clapped Boone on the shoulder. "We have the same shoe size. Remember?"

"I'll get them," Grace said. "This worked out perfectly. Didn't it, Boone?"

The minute Grace walked away, Boone turned toward Declan. "You know you're going to pay for this, don't you?" Boone said through clenched teeth.

"I figured as much," Declan said. "But watching Grace teach you to skate will be well worth it."

Grace made her way back to them, lugging Declan's

skating bag. She had a pleased expression on her face. "Here we go, Boone. Let's put on your skates."

The excitement etched on Grace's face, combined with the enthusiasm oozing from her voice, was undeniable. Seeing her like this—joyful, eager and full of anticipation—was worth a little discomfort on his part. The thought of getting out on the ice for the first time felt a little intimidating, but he was going to embrace it for all it was worth. Because it made her radiant with happiness. Because it mattered to Grace. And the knowledge swept over him like the cold blast of an artic wind. Suddenly, what meant the world to Grace, deeply mattered to him, as well.

As Grace led him onto the ice in front of half the town, Boone uttered a fervent prayer. *Please don't let me make a fool of myself in front of Grace.*

After an hour on the ice, Grace knew it was time to give Boone a reprieve. For a novice, he'd done a great job, even though he'd taken a few hard falls. His cords were covered in frosty ice. In the end, he managed to skate around the ice with her in a somewhat wobbly fashion. She gave him high points for effort and his can-do attitude.

"You were great," she said as they made their way off the ice.

Boone shot her a look of disbelief. "Seriously? If I fell any more I'd have been mopping up the ice."

Grace tried to hide her laughter behind her mittened hand. "Your attitude was great. Every time you fell, you got right back up."

"Of course I did. Can't have my date thinking I'm soft," Boone said with a little bit of swagger in his voice.

Boone practically collapsed onto a wooden bench. He flung his arms out to the side and threw his head back, sticking his tongue out. "I think I'll just stay here for the rest of the night," Boone said.

"Hey! Look alive, Boone. If we hurry up and take our skates off we can beat the rush for the hot apple cider," Grace said, darting a glance toward the concessions line. The line wasn't too crazy at the moment, and the cider would be the perfect way to take the chill out of their bones. Although she thought he looked mighty cute, Boone's nose was as red as a strawberry.

After hearing her suggestion, Boone bent down and quickly took off Declan's skates. He heaved a huge sigh as soon as he put on his own boots. As they walked toward the concession stand, they met up with Gunther and Wanda, who were standing in line.

Gunther beamed as Wanda stood next to him, her arm looped through his. They looked like an old married couple.

Gunther called out to them in greeting. "Hey, Boone. Grace. Looking good out there."

"Hey, Gunther. Wanda. You're too kind," Boone drawled. "Gracie was doing all the heavy lifting, keeping me on my feet."

"Stop being so humble. You were incredible," Grace raved. "I still can't believe it was your first time out on the ice. You're a natural."

"You two were both great," said Wanda. "Let's hope we glide out there as well as these two," Wanda said with a laugh. Gunther leaned in and tightly clutched Wanda's hand. They gazed into each other's eyes as if they were the only two people in the universe. Grace watched the couple as they walked off with cups of cider in their hands.

"I sure hope it all works out between them," Grace said with a rueful shake of her head as she reached out for the cup of apple cider Boone purchased.

"This is the second time you've made mention of people not getting their hopes up about love," Boone remarked. He was staring at her intently.

She shrugged. "I think people ought to tread carefully where love is concerned. That's all."

Boone leaned in toward her and asked in a low voice, "Are you guarding your heart, Gracie?"

"If I don't guard it, who will?" she snapped.

Boone stopped in his tracks. When she looked over at him he was gazing at her with a look of dismay etched on his face.

"What happened to you? Who made you so reluctant to put your heart out there?" His soulful eyes flickered over her face. Boone's question created an immediate reaction inside her. It was like poking a grizzly bear with a stick. She didn't want to go to that dark place of hurt she'd lived in for so long. If she did, there was a danger she might never crawl back out.

She rolled her eyes. "You're not going there, are you?"

He leaned in toward her so that his arresting face was mere inches from her own. Her nostrils twitched at the woodsy scent of him. She wanted to swat him away like a pesky gnat. He was getting too close, in more ways than one. He was opening up old, painful wounds.

"Who hurt you, Gracie?" Boone's voice was low and tender.

"No one," she mumbled. "Nothing."

"What happened?" he pressed.

"I grew up. That's what happened," she said in a curt tone.

He narrowed his eyes. "So you stopped believing in happily-ever-after?"

She let out an indelicate snort. "Humph. Happily-ever-after is a fairy tale. No prince is going to go door to door looking for me with a glass slipper in his hand."

He raised his brow. "And you say this because?" The tone of his voice was incredulous.

"I was supposed to get married, if you really want to know. Right before the wedding, he told me he'd fallen in love with someone else." She hadn't meant to tell him, hadn't wanted to confide something so personal. "I didn't even have time to run from the church with my tail between my legs. So unless you've stood up in a church full of people and explained to them that your wedding has been called off by your groom—" Her voice trailed off, swallowed up by raw emotion.

Boone's eyes began to blink rapidly. His mouth opened and then shut. Finally, he spoke, his voice sounding raspy. "Someone left you at the altar?"

"Yes. My college sweetheart, Trey. Turns out he wasn't so sweet."

Boone didn't laugh. He gazed at her with an expression that threatened to strip away the last of her composure. She didn't need pity, and she didn't need sorrow on her behalf!

She blinked away the moisture in her eyes. After all this time she couldn't believe she was getting emotional about it. She'd put a lid on these feelings two years ago. "It was an hour before I was to walk down the aisle."

Her stomach clenched as all the memories rolled through her. Even now, some twenty-six months later, she still felt the embarrassment of that moment. Shame still coursed through her at the notion that she hadn't been good enough. Trey Walker III hadn't wanted her as his wife. His intention hadn't been to crush her, of that she'd been certain. But he hadn't wanted to commit himself to a woman he didn't love. What he'd felt for her hadn't been the type of love that would last a lifetime.

It wasn't his fault he'd fallen in love with someone else. He'd been caught up in a terrible dilemma. The choice had been between obligation to her and following his heart's desire. He'd chosen to follow his heart, making her a casualty in the process.

As a result, her family had turned their backs on her. And ever since, she'd felt achingly alone.

And now Boone was poking and prodding at a wound that still wasn't fully healed, even though she'd almost convinced herself that everything was fine.

"So pardon me for doubting whether love can last a lifetime, because mine didn't even last long enough to make it down the aisle." Although she'd thrown the words out there in a defiant way, her voice came out shaky and uncertain, mirroring the way she felt on the inside.

Boone's brown eyes flickered. His expression softened. "But you're here, so you must still believe in love."

Guilt speared through her upon hearing Boone's words. Love had nothing to do with it. For her, coming to Alaska had been all about business. She'd known that by covering this story and writing her series she'd be in line for professional accolades at the *Tribune*. She'd make a name for herself in journalistic circles. Maybe even get a promotion. But not for anything in this world could she ever admit that to Boone.

"Yes, I'm here," she said in small voice. "For what it's worth."

He reached out and wrapped her mittened hand in his gloved one. "It's worth a lot, Gracie. Believing in something when everything tells you it might not be worth believing in...that's faith."

She shook her head. It didn't seem right to allow him to think she was a woman of faith. It was bad enough that Boone believed she was in Alaska in the pursuit of a romantic relationship. God hadn't been a part of her life since her world had fallen apart two years ago. He'd stood by and let her whole world crumble into dust.

"I haven't believed in anything for a very long time," she admitted in a small voice.

Boone squeezed her hand tightly. "I'm so sorry that your hopes and dreams were crushed. I understand what it feels like to have your world fall apart around you. My heart has been knocked around a time or two, but I still have faith. I still believe in loving someone with every fiber of my being. And even though my trust has been broken, I still want everlasting love. I think I deserve that."

She tried to swallow past the huge lump in her throat. Boone's words had reached deep down inside her very soul and tugged hard on her heartstrings. The feelings he was stirring up were powerful. If she had to reduce it to one single emotion, it was longing. Deep, profound longing. He'd tapped into the very core of her beliefs—the ones she kept hidden behind a thick, impenetrable wall. Hiding them had been a whole lot easier than grieving the loss of her dreams. The loss of her family. The future she'd dreamed of ever since she was a kid—Trey and enough children to fill up a huge Victorian house in the suburbs.

When her wedding had come apart at the seams, her family had acted as if she was their shame, their disappointment, their soul-crushing moment. Instead of taking her into the fold and nursing away the hurt, they'd treated her like an albatross around their necks. They'd blamed her for botching an opportunity to improve their social standing.

The words her mother had hurled at her would be imprinted in her memory forever.

"All you had to do was get him to walk down the aisle, and you couldn't even do that right."

She flinched as the callousness of her mother's words served as a reminder of her fractured family and the hole in her that might never be filled up. She hadn't deserved their treatment, nor their scorn. They should have loved her all the more, no matter how disappointed they felt.

"I suppose I am guarding my heart. It's hard to believe in anything when the people who are supposed to love you unconditionally turn their backs on you and break your heart into a hundred little pieces in the process."

Chapter Nine

The pain etched on Grace's face nearly did him in. Her words rocked him to his core. A mighty anger began brewing inside him. This Trey character was weak and unprincipled. And her family should have provided her with open arms and a soft place to fall. They should have rallied around her and closed ranks until her wounds healed. From the sounds of it, she'd been thrown under the bus by everyone involved. He hurt terribly for her.

He felt nothing but disgust for Trey! He battled an urge to book a flight to New York City just so he could face this coward and give him a piece of his mind. What kind of man allowed a woman to think they were getting married and then tossed her aside right before they were supposed to meet at the altar and exchange their vows before their loved ones and God?

Boone cleared his throat. He needed to get a handle on this and figure out what he was up against. Perhaps Grace had come to Love in order to get over her ex-fiancé. There was a distinct possibility that she still had strong feelings for him. Cameron was a prime example.

Despite Paige's machinations, his brother still loved her. And Honor still hadn't gotten over Joshua.

"Do you still love him?" There was no sense in beating around the bush. If she was still in love with her spineless ex, he needed to know before he invested any more of himself in Grace.

She didn't answer for a moment, and he felt his heart drop to his stomach. *Please, don't be in love with him.* The thought repeated in his head like a benediction. He stared into those vivid blue eyes of hers, hoping he might find his answer in their depths.

"No, I don't love him," she answered with a hint of a smile perched on her lips. "And to tell you the truth, I'm not sure I ever really did. Not in the truest sense of the word. He represented something to me that I'd been yearning for my whole life."

"Acceptance?" he asked. It seemed clear to him that the people in Grace's life hadn't shown her unconditional love. Perhaps Grace had believed that in marrying Trey, her family would finally accept her.

Surprise flashed in her eyes. "Yes. I suppose that was a large part of it. Wide-open arms to embrace me when the world gets crazy all around me."

"There are plenty of arms that can do that. You just have to know where to look to find them," Boone drawled.

Their gazes met and held. Understanding passed between them. Grace's shoulders relaxed. She let out a little sigh. Her defenses were down. She was no longer fighting him. Now he knew exactly why she'd been so prickly and why she doubted Operation Love. She hadn't wanted Gunther, Lionel or Abel to get hurt because she herself had been badly bruised by love. Being aware of

Grace's past made him feel even closer to her. They'd both invested themselves in people who weren't worthy of their devotion.

"That's good to know," Grace murmured.

Boone felt a tad guilt-ridden about the speech he'd just delivered to Grace. Here he was spouting off about believing in love when he himself was holding back. He'd been shielding his heart against Grace from day one. That all was going to end tonight. He was going to take a step out of his comfort zone and show Grace that he wasn't just paying lip service. He intended to show her in no uncertain terms that he was wide-open to all the possibilities.

As she stood and looked down at the townsfolk gathered around Deer Run Lake, Grace felt a sense of peace envelop her. So many nights she'd lain awake praying for this very feeling. She'd asked God for closure and tranquillity. Now, unexpectedly, she'd found serenity in the most unlikely of places. And she knew a large part of it was due to Boone. Every moment she spent in his company helped restore her belief in finding someone who shared similar beliefs about life and love and family.

She'd shocked herself by being so open with Boone about her romantic past. It wasn't something she normally shared. And he'd been sensitive and tender and kind. When he'd talked about faith, he'd made her feel as if it was still a part of her, even though she hadn't recognized it until now.

It was becoming crystal clear to her that she needed to lead a more faith-driven life. And even though she'd turned her back on God, He was continually showing her that He hadn't given up on her.

Lord, I need to believe in something. I want to trust in a higher power, to know that no matter what happens I can lean on You, Lord. For so long now I've been winging it on my own. All it's gotten me is loneliness. And for so long I've been pretending to have it all, when in reality I'm lacking the very things I want the most.

A sudden roar went up in the throng of people. The crowd began to buzz noisily.

"Look, Grace," Boone shouted as he pointed up at the sky. "If you live to be a hundred you might never see anything half as beautiful as this."

Northern lights. She let out a gasp as a myriad of colors undulated across the sky. Greens. White. A splash of red appeared. Violet streaks of light shimmered across the sky.

She tilted her head back and stared up at the heavens in wonder. "How is this happening?"

Boone's explanation came swiftly. "It's a storm of sorts. The effect comes from energy surging down the earth's magnetic field. Our ancestors thought it was past and future events being displayed across the sky."

She raised her hand toward the vibrating lights. It felt as if she might be able to reach out and grab hold of the bright, flashing waves.

"It's magnificent," she said. It was almost as if a painter had made a canvas of the sky and splashed paint all over the heavens.

"Beautiful," Boone said with a sigh.

When she turned toward him, his eyes were focused solely on her. He wasn't even gazing at the aurora borealis. He reached for her hand and clutched it tightly. Their arms were touching, and even though layers separated them, she felt an electric charge as they brushed against each other. Boone was looking at her with such wonder and appreciation it made her knees almost buckle underneath her.

He pulled her close, dipping his head down and capturing her lips in a wonderful, tender kiss that took her breath away. Despite the cold, his lips were warm and toasty. A groundswell of emotion surged up inside her. For someone whose heart had felt frozen for entirely too long, this kiss demonstrated that she was rapidly coming back to life. As his lips moved over hers she couldn't help but wish it might go on forever. She leaned in closer and kissed him back with everything she had stored up inside her. Every hope. Every dream. Every wish made its way into the kiss.

As the kiss ended she felt Boone's bare hands moving through her hair before sliding down to caress the side of her face and neck.

"Gracie," Boone murmured. "I've been wanting to do that since the first time I saw you."

She couldn't stop herself from grinning, even though a little voice told her to keep it cool.

"The first time we met I kind of thought you were a wet blanket."

Boone arched an eyebrow. "Seriously?" She nodded her head, stifling a chuckle. "But I saved you from slipping on the ice."

She planted her hands on her hips. "And you criticized my shoes and failed to appreciate my song."

Boone threw his head back and roared with laughter. "The 'Sheriff of Love' song? I thought you were making fun of me."

Grace shook her hand at him. "You need to learn to appreciate quirkiness."

She snuck a glance over at the ice, wondering if Boone would be game for another go-round. A tall, sturdy-looking man with a pint-size companion immediately drew her attention. The little munchkin was tugging the man toward the ice.

"Boone," she cried out. "It's Liam. And Aidan."

Boone followed the direction of her gaze, his face lighting up when he spotted them. "Wow. I can't believe they came! Let's go say hello," Boone said, his voice laced with enthusiasm as he grabbed her hand and they made their way over to the lake's perimeter.

By the time they reached Liam and Aidan, a storm was brewing between father and son. Aidan had his arms folded across his small chest. His eyes flashed warning signs.

"Hey, buddy. What's that pout all about?" Boone asked as he swung his nephew into his arms.

"I want to go skate, but Daddy says no," Aidan said, his lip jutting out as tears pooled in his eyes.

Liam let out a ragged sigh. "Aidan, there's nothing more I'd like to do than take you skating, but Daddy never learned how. You need to learn from someone who knows what they're doing."

"I want to use my new skates," Aidan sobbed. He pointed to the dark brown pair of skates in his father's hand.

Grace leaned over and grabbed hold of Aidan's chubby hand. "How would you like it if I took you out there on the ice? I love to skate."

Aidan stared at her with big brown eyes. His little brows were knitted together.

Boone whispered loudly in his ear, "And she's a terrific skater, too. She'll whip you around the ice like lightning."

Aidan's eyes widened even farther. "Whoa. Lightning," he said. Turning toward Grace he said, "I wanna skate with you."

Grace held out her hand. "I'm Grace. Nice to meet you, Aidan."

"How do you know my name?" Aidan asked in a stunned voice.

"I was at your house the other night when you woke up and came into the living room. Your daddy was fixing me up."

"Oh. Uncle Boone's lady."

Uncle Boone's lady? Her face flushed at Aidan's comment. Boone couldn't have grinned wider. Both he and Liam chuckled.

"Why don't we get your skates on, Aidan?" Liam told his son. He turned toward Grace with a grateful smile. "Thanks so much. He would never have let me live it down if he didn't get to skate tonight."

"My pleasure," Grace said, feeling happy that she'd done a little something to help Liam and his adorable son. She couldn't imagine how difficult it must be to raise a little one after losing your spouse.

Once Aidan had his skates on, Grace took him out to the ice. Sophie waved to her enthusiastically from a few feet away as she skated with a group of admirers. Bending down at the waist, she took Aidan's hands in hers and began to slowly lead him around the rink. She was skating backward, which earned her a few surprised glances. She'd learned this trick at an early age, and it was the best way to teach Aidan how to glide around the ice without taking her eyes off him. He seemed surprised to be gliding around the ice. His joyful laughter filled her soul with happiness. There was nothing quite so innocent as a child's laugh. As she let go of Aidan's hands and watched him take a few fledgling steps on his own, she heard the whistles and shouts of praise from the sidelines. Aidan resembled a newborn colt just getting his legs. Boone and Liam were standing there, cheering Aidan on. Boone smiled in their direction—a sweet, tender smile—that nestled its way into her heart.

She didn't want this wonderful evening to end. Being with Boone tonight had brought her indescribable joy. Teaching him how to skate and seeing the stunning northern lights were memories she would carry around with her forever. Sharing a kiss with Boone as the sky lit up with nature's beauty had been the most romantic moment of her life. And being out on the lake with Aidan made her think about someday holding her own kids in her arms.

The residents of Love had made her feel like one of their own. And even though she'd promised herself not to get in too deep, it was too late. Between a swoon-worthy sheriff and a town full of eccentric, lovable folks who embraced her with open arms, her heart was growing by leaps and bounds. It was no longer her own. With that knowledge came a little fear. She'd already had the rug pulled out from her when Trey changed his mind about marrying her. The thought of being hurt by Boone scared her. And there was nothing she could do to stop this relationship from going further. It was far too late to rein her feelings in. She was falling head over heels in love with Sheriff Boone Prescott.

* * *

By the time morning came, Boone's backside and legs were hurting. His falls on the ice had left him with some aches and pains that were difficult to ignore. He had no regrets, though. His date with Grace had been a memorable one. Thoughts of the romantic kiss they'd shared had been at the forefront of his mind ever since he woke up. Finding out about her past gave him a good idea as to why she'd ventured all the way to Alaska. She was looking for a fresh start. It was an opportunity to reinvent herself away from her family and ex-fiancé.

It must have been difficult to deal with the stares and whispers in the weeks and months following the canceled wedding. Even in a small town like Love, gossip was insidious. Being here, he imagined, allowed Grace to rewrite the story of her life. He just hoped there was a place for him in her life, because he was starting to think of Grace as a permanent fixture in his.

He whistled a happy tune as he pulled up outside Liam's house carrying an armful of groceries. It still wasn't easy for Liam to be out and about in public. Last night had been a rare exception, and he'd only showed up at the ice-skating social for Aidan's sake. He felt a gigantic smile breaking out over his face as the memory of Grace and Aidan skating together washed over him. It was nice knowing she had such a way with children. Aidan had been putty in her hands.

When the door slowly opened, Aidan was standing at the threshold, a shy smile on his face.

"Uncle Boone. Uncle Boone." He grabbed him by the legs and peered behind him. "Where's Grace?"

"She's not here, buddy. I'm pretty sure she's working

with Uncle Cam today." He lifted the grocery bags in the air. "What am I, chopped liver?"

Aidan stuck out his tongue. "Yucky. I hate liver."

Liam's voice called to him from inside the house. "Come on in, Boone. We're in the kitchen." With Aidan leading the way, Boone walked toward the back of the house. The brightly lit kitchen, all white with granite counter tops, had been the handiwork of Ruby, Liam's deceased wife. It was an airy, cheerful room that belied the current circumstances of Liam's family. As soon as he crossed the threshold, the scent of freshly baked bread rose to his nostrils. Honor and Liam were standing at the stove putting the finishing touches on a pizza fresh out of the oven.

"You're just in time. Take a seat. We're just slicing it now," Liam explained.

As everyone sat down, Boone noticed Liam's none-too-subtle maneuvering that placed him right next to his sister. Honor barely glanced in his direction, letting him know the frostiness between them still hadn't thawed. He was beginning to think she might never warm up toward him.

Liam placed the pizza in the middle of the table and began serving up piping hot slices.

"Reindeer sausage pizza. I love reindeer pizza," Aidan shouted. His chubby hand was raised triumphantly in the air.

"You've gotten good at making this," Boone noted between bites of pizza.

"I had to," Liam said with a shuttered expression. "Ruby was always the chef in this house. I had to learn on the fly once she was gone. It's Aidan's favorite."

Honor shot Boone a dirty glance, as if letting him

know he shouldn't have brought up the subject of cooking. As if he'd been responsible for Liam's mind straying toward Ruby. At this point, Honor blamed him for everything under the sun, and he was getting mighty sick and tired of it. With an angry huff he placed his napkin on the table and stood up. He pointed in Honor's direction. "You. And me. Living room. Now."

"I—I'm eating right now," she sputtered, looking over at Liam for support.

"Go on, Honor. You've run from this long enough," Liam said.

Aidan looked back and forth between them with a curious expression on his face. He'd just stuffed a big piece of crust in his mouth. Honor stood up abruptly and pushed back her chair. With her arms folded across her chest, she marched to the living room.

She turned on her heel to face him. "What is it?" she snapped, her eyes flashing fire.

Boone folded his arms across his chest and stared Honor down. "For starters, I would appreciate it if you'd speak to me with some measure of respect. If you expect to be treated like a grown woman, you need to act like one."

Honor's cheeks flushed and she gazed down at the hardwood floors. "I'm sorry," she mumbled.

"Second, I owe you an apology," Boone said.

Honor slowly lifted her head up. Her mouth hung open. "A what? An apology?"

"Yes. An apology," he repeated.

Honor gaped at him. Her gray-blue eyes flickered.

"Come on. Don't act like I've never apologized before."

She slowly nodded her head. "Maybe once when we were kids."

"I was wrong in the way I handled things," he admitted. "The other night Grace made me realize how I never acknowledged your pain or the heartache you went through. She was right. I was so busy making sure you didn't marry Joshua that I ran right over you and your feelings in the process. And in doing so, I harmed our relationship. I know it pained you to end things with Joshua. I know you loved him. And I'm sorry if it gives you pain to know he married someone else.

"I love you, Honor. To this day, one of the happiest moments in my life is the day Mom and Dad brought you home from the hospital. I couldn't fathom that something so beautiful and perfect belonged to us. I don't want to be on opposite sides of the fence anymore. All I want is my sister back."

Honor rushed at him, landing with a thud against his chest. She began crying and talking incoherently. "I've missed you, Boone," she said. He put his arms around her and held her tight. He raised his hand and stroked her hair the way he'd done when she was a little girl. She smelled of sunshine and roses and sweetness.

She looked at him somberly, her eyes red rimmed with emotion. "You can't go through life judging people, Boone. Even though Joshua made a lot of mistakes, he was a good person. And you couldn't see that… You were blind to it. Promise me you won't make that mistake again."

"I promise you, I won't." He reached out and tugged her finger the same way he'd done ever since she was little They locked gazes. "I'm a different man these days, Honor. I don't see things through the same narrow lens."

Honor smiled at him, a genuine, contented smile that reminded him of her youthful self. It gave him a pang to see her like this after such an agonizing estrangement. Hope for their renewed relationship burgeoned inside him. With God, all things were possible, he reminded himself.

His sister reached for his other hand and led him back toward the kitchen. Liam stared at their joined hands and grinned so hard it threatened to crack his face.

"Well done," Liam said with a nod of his head.

Once lunch was finished, Honor volunteered to do the dishes while Boone caught up with Liam. Aidan settled into playing with his blocks while Boone and Liam sat in the living room.

"I'm so glad you decided to come out the other night to the skating party," Boone said, a smile tugging at his lips at the memory of Aidan on the ice.

"I'm not sure I was ready to be at a social gathering, but seeing Aidan out there having the time of his life was priceless." Liam reached out and clasped his shoulder. "Thanks for inviting us."

"Any opportunity to be surrounded by my family, and I'm going to grab it with both hands," Boone said.

"After the skating party we stopped by to visit with Jasper for a spell," Liam said. "I wanted to take a look at that ankle and make sure it was healing properly."

Boone nodded, wishing he'd had time last night to check on Jasper. "I haven't seen him for a few days. How's it holding up?"

"It's healing up nicely, although it was a bad break. His bones aren't what they used to be, due to his age. But he's getting around pretty well on the crutches."

"That's good to hear," he said, happy to know that his

grandfather was on the mend. "He really had no business being out there at the cave. I wish he could finally lay all that legend lore to rest."

"What's worse is that he hasn't been taking his medicine," Liam added.

"The statins for his heart?" Boone asked.

"Yes," Liam said in a solemn voice. "And he really needs to keep taking them, as well as adjusting his diet and exercising."

Boone bit the inside of his lip. "What you're saying is that he's at risk for another cardiac episode if he doesn't straighten up his act."

"Yep. That's what I think," Liam said. "He needs to start taking his conditions seriously instead of creeping around in caves chasing gold."

Liam's thoughts mirrored his own. Hearing it confirmed by a medical doctor cemented his opinion that Jasper needed to rein in his activities and make a few lifestyle changes. No more burgers and fries or corn dogs.

Boone realized he needed to take a more active role in Jasper's health. "When I get back to town I'm going to swing by and see him at his office. We have a town council meeting tonight, so I'll make it seem as if I want to talk to him about the town budget. I won't let him know we talked."

Liam shot him a wary glance. "Don't go overboard, Boone. You tend to barrel in like a bull at a rodeo. This needs to be handled delicately, otherwise Jasper will just dig his heels in and refuse to budge."

"I promise to tread lightly," he said, realizing that both of his siblings had garnered a promise from him during this visit. He intended on honoring them both.

"He's awful fond of your friend Grace," Liam said. "Aidan and I think she's pretty amazing, as well."

Boone felt a rush of pleasure at the notion that his family had given Grace their stamp of approval. It matched up with the way he felt about her. She was delightful in every way. Funny. Sweet. Beautiful. And kind. And he got the feeling she was looking for the same things he was seeking. A strong, faithful partner. Wide-open arms to embrace her. A love for all time.

"I think if Jasper was a few years younger, he'd make a play for her," Boone said with a chuckle.

"Who's to say he won't?" Liam said with a shake of his head. "He told me they were doing some treasure hunting today. Maybe he has a little crush on her."

Treasure hunting. Grace and Jasper? No. It wasn't possible. He'd already explained to Grace that enabling Jasper in his pursuit of the town legend wasn't healthy for his grandfather. And she'd promised him that she wouldn't do anything to encourage him any further. Liam must have misunderstood. Grace wouldn't go back on her word.

"Are you sure about that?" he pressed. He was getting a funny feeling in his insides. Little prickles of awareness rose up on his arms. That sensation usually heralded bad news. He shook it off, realizing he was jumping to conclusions.

Liam nodded. "He went on and on about it. Said he was ordering lunch at his office for the two of them so they could map out some stuff."

Map out some stuff? Such as another location to go treasure hunting? He stuffed down a burst of annoyance. He needed to reserve judgment until he knew something concrete. Hadn't he just promised Honor to be more flexible and less unyielding?

Boone glanced at his watch. Perhaps if he headed back to town right away he'd be able to see what Jasper was up to and allay some of his concerns about his grandfather. After abruptly saying his goodbyes to his family and promising to take Aidan sledding on the weekend, Boone got in his cruiser and headed back to town. His first stop was the mayor's office. As much as he told himself his main interest was assessing his grandfather and his well-being, another part of him knew that he was also checking in on Grace. He uttered a quick prayer that his faith in her hadn't been misguided.

Chapter Ten

Sitting on the floor of the mayor's office with maps and diagrams spread out all around her made Grace feel like an adventurer. Truthfully, this was even more fun than their spelunking escapade, especially since it didn't involve her freezing her tootsies off. And she'd managed to keep her promise to Boone. Looking at maps of Love with Jasper wasn't treasure hunting, and it wasn't putting him in any danger. It was simply spending time with a friend who badly needed a shoulder to lean on.

The truth was, Jasper was lonely. When he'd invited her to have lunch with him in his office a few days ago under the guise of showing her an antique map of Love, she'd agreed on the spot.

She didn't have the heart to cancel on him, especially since he told her no one else wanted to entertain his talk about Bodine Prescott's treasure. Grace had come to the conclusion that for Jasper the treasure represented something he needed to cling to, like a beacon of hope for the hometown he loved so dearly.

Hope couldn't be a bad thing.

When Grace had arrived at his office, she'd made it

clear that her spelunking days were over. Jasper said he understood, but he still wanted to show her some potential spots for the location of the treasure.

Grace had her notebook out and was scribbling down some notes for Jasper. Something was niggling at her, some fact they'd come across that didn't compute. It was hovering on the edge of her brain, but she couldn't connect the dots.

"Jasper, what year did Bodine and his brother drown out on the bay?"

Jasper scratched at his chin, a thoughtful expression etched on his face. "Hmm...must have been not long after he found the gold in Juneau. Eighteen eighty-one, I believe." Grace wrote the date down on the page, along with the year he'd discovered gold. She was working on a timeline.

"Was it his own boat?" she asked.

"I assume so, but to be honest, I don't rightly know," he admitted.

Again, Grace scribbled down that tidbit of information.

"Grace, I want to show you a picture of my wife." The tone of Jasper's voice quieted and softened. It sounded as gentle as a caress. He reached over to his desk and carefully picked up a picture frame. Jasper extended it to her and she let out a gasp at the fragile beauty who stared back at her. The woman in the picture had long dark hair and gray-blue eyes. There was a look of sadness in her eyes, as well as a determination that resonated with the strong tilt of her jaw.

"That was my wife, Harmony."

"Oh, she was lovely. And she looked happy," Grace remarked.

"Most beautiful woman I'd ever laid eyes on. God-fearing, too. And the most humble. That woman had no idea how stunning she was or how many men in town were crazy about her." He grinned and pointed a thumb at his own chest. "But she picked me. Me. Proudest moment of my life."

"Sounds like a love match," Grace said, knowing the story was bittersweet due to its ending.

"It was. Until it wasn't." Jasper let out a sigh. "Always remember to hold on to love, Grace. Never let it go."

"If it ever happens for me, I promise to cherish it," Grace said, her thoughts straying toward Boone.

Jasper winked at her. "Rumor has it you've been spending a bit of time with my grandson."

Grace laughed. "Uh-oh. Boone and I are the topic of town gossip?"

"Don't let that bother you none. People have been waiting a long time to see Boone come out of his romantic funk." He reached out and clutched her hand. "He's a good man, Grace. As solid as they come. Gruff on the outside, but as tender and kindhearted as a lamb on the inside. He'd make a nice father, too."

"Jasper? Are you playing matchmaker?" Grace asked, buoyed by the wonderful things Jasper had told her about Boone. She'd already figured out what kind of man Boone was, but it was nice to hear Jasper corroborate her opinion.

Instead of answering, Jasper winced and began rubbing his chest.

"Hey. What is it? Did the food not agree with you?" Jasper had ordered some sandwiches and side dishes for their lunch, along with two cans of cream soda and two éclairs for dessert. They'd gobbled everything up in record time.

Jasper pressed a hand to his head. "I'm not feeling so good all of a sudden. Something in my chest feels tight."

Grace scrambled to her feet. "Let me get you some water." She quickly went over to Jasper's water cooler and filled a plastic cup to the brim with ice-cold water. Grace walked back toward Jasper and held the cup up to his lips. "Take small sips," she instructed.

The door to the mayor's office abruptly flew open, right before Boone marched into Jasper's office, his face as stormy as a thundercloud.

The moment he stepped in to the mayor's private office, Boone realized that his belief in Grace might have been misplaced. Not only was she in Jasper's office, but the floor was scattered with maps and notebooks. There was no doubt in his mind that Grace was Jasper's sidekick, despite her promise not to encourage his grandfather in his dreams of rivers of gold flowing through Love.

He drew his brows together. Something was going on with Jasper. He didn't look so great. "What's wrong?" Boone blurted out.

"He's not feeling well. He was having a pain in his chest," Grace explained, a look of concern radiating in her eyes.

Boone strode forward and leaned over so he was eye to eye with his grandfather.

"Do I need to take you to the clinic? Does it feel like you're having a heart attack?" Boone asked in a gentle voice.

"I think it's just gas," he said with a sheepish look. "I thought it was my heart for a second."

"Are you sure?" Boone asked. "Sometimes the symptoms are hard to pinpoint."

"I'm sure. My stomach is all bubbly and making funny noises," Jasper explained. "It's my stomach, not my chest. Thank the Lord for small mercies."

Boone felt beads of perspiration gather on his forehead. He swiped them away with the back of his hand. He'd felt a sense of rising panic before Jasper had dispelled his fears.

"I'm going to mosey down the hall so I can raid the first-aid kit for some antacid," Jasper said.

"You sure you're okay?" Boone reached out and helped Jasper with his crutches. He held his arm to steady him.

Jasper shrugged off Boone's hand. "I said I'm fine. Don't treat me like an invalid." He wagged his eyebrows in Grace's direction. "I'm sure you two lovebirds won't mind a few moments alone." Jasper swung himself on his crutches toward the door. Boone held his breath as Jasper maneuvered the opening and closing of his office door.

Boone turned back toward Grace. "What's going on here?" He darted a glance at the materials scattered on the floor. It was fairly shocking that Jasper had nothing better to do as town mayor than to research the family legend. And Grace had given up her lunch hour to help him!

Grace shrugged. "Nothing much. We were just having a little fun. Jasper was showing me on the map where your ancestor Bodine went down with his ship."

Part of him knew he shouldn't take out his frustrations on Grace, but he was so sick and tired of hearing about gold and buried treasure and legends. He'd grown up hearing about it and he knew how Jasper's obsession had been one of the factors in the dissolution of his grandparents' marriage. He couldn't help but think it had trickled down to his own parents' marriage. At what point did it all end?

He shook his head. "Fun? Was that before or after he started having chest pains?"

Grace's eyes flickered with surprise. "He ate too much or too quickly. You heard him. It's gas."

Boone folded his arms across his chest and began tapping his foot. "Am I wrong here, or did you agree not to get involved with Jasper's legend theories? I seem to recall a certain promise you made to me."

Grace wrinkled her nose. Her eyes flashed with surprise. "I kept my word. We didn't go treasure hunting. Jasper just showed me some old maps and a few diagrams. I acted as a sounding board. Nothing more."

"You're encouraging him." Boone knew his words sounded like an accusation, but more and more it was beginning to sound as if Grace might actually believe in the legend herself. That would only make things worse.

Grace cocked her head to the side and gazed at him curiously. "Boone, you seem upset with me, and I don't know why. We were having fun. I don't think there's anything wrong with having a little joy in the middle of a humdrum day."

"Grace, this might be some fun little diversion for you, but it means a whole lot more to him."

Grace visibly bristled. "Oh, I know what it means to him. He's made it very clear to me…along with the fact that no one in his family listens to him or takes him seriously. Jasper thinks by finding the treasure he can help the town financially. He wants to save his hometown. That's his big dream."

Boone shook his head in disbelief. Was she suddenly an expert on Jasper? Was she really trying to make it seem as if she knew more about his grandfather than his own family? And to suggest that no one listened to him, when they'd been doing so for decades. She had no clue, he imagined, how close they'd come to losing him with his cardiac episode last year. He bit the inside of his cheek to stop himself from saying something he might regret.

"What you don't know is that Jasper has been chasing this legend ever since he was a kid. His obsession with it was one of the reasons my grandmother left him. He's lost a lot because of this single-minded pursuit. Last year he had a heart attack. And having a little fun shouldn't place his health in jeopardy," Boone explained in a curt tone.

Grace's mouth swung open. "I would never place him in harm's way. You're blowing this all out of proportion. I care about your grandfather. "

"If you cared about him you wouldn't be sitting here on the floor scanning maps with him!" he snapped. "Isn't it bad enough Jasper broke his ankle? What's next? Toppling down some stairs or another heart attack?"

All the color suddenly leached out of Grace's peaches-and-cream complexion. "I wouldn't let anything happen to him."

"Well, Grace. Something already happened and you couldn't stop it. Could you?"

"It was an accident," she said in a soft voice. She paused for a moment as if she was struggling to keep her composure. "I know you want to protect everyone in your family from getting hurt, but you can't lock them up in a tower to do it. Jasper isn't an invalid, and he's not a child. You need to let him live his life."

Boone felt his chest getting tight. An accident was how Liam had lost Ruby. His own father had been severely injured in that same avalanche rescue operation. "Were you here when Jasper had his heart attack? Or when he got so consumed by legend hunting that my grandmother left him? You can't just show up here in Love acting like you have all the answers."

A look of hurt passed over her face before she quickly shuttered her expression. After grabbing her notebook, she scrambled to her feet and snatched her purse from the edge of Jasper's desk. Without a word of goodbye, she stalked out of the room, leaving a huge void in her wake and a feeling of discord lingering in the air.

As soon as Grace left, Boone propped himself against Jasper's desk, his entire body sagging as he exhaled. Although it had felt good in the moment to unleash all his worries, he didn't feel right about lashing out at Grace. She'd been a scapegoat for all his pent-up feelings about Jasper's health and the angst of his siblings. Now, with a few careless words, he might have ruined the best thing that had ever happened to him. And he had no idea how to make things right.

Returning to the Moose Café and finishing her shift took all the composure in the world for Grace. She should have been awarded an Oscar for smiling and making pleasantries with customers while her mind was swirling with chaos. In a few sentences Boone had reduced her to a careless, thoughtless airhead, who butted her nose in his family's' business and placed Jasper in danger. And she'd barely fought back. Tears stung her eyes as she tried to push Boone's words out of her mind.

So much for the romantic kiss they'd shared or the

feelings that were blossoming between them. Why in the world had she fallen for one of the most arrogant, opinionated men in Alaska?

"What's wrong, Grace?" Sophie cornered her in the kitchen, placing her arm around her shoulder and peering into her eyes. "You don't look so hot."

"I don't feel so good," she said, placing her hand across her belly.

"Did something you ate disagree with you?" Sophie asked, concern etched on her face.

"Something disagreed with me all right," she mumbled. "I'm going to lie down for a bit as soon as we get back to the cabins."

The whole ride back to the Black Bear Cabins, Sophie and Hazel tried to engage her in conversation, but Grace couldn't focus on talk of ice fishing and sledding at Deer Run Lake. A slow fury was building up inside her like a volcano on the cusp of bubbling over. With a halfhearted wave to her friends, she let herself into her cabin.

Anger beat a fast path through her as she stalked backed and forth across the hardwood floors in her cabin. Tears of frustration pooled in her eyes, but she wouldn't allow herself to cry. Frankly, Sheriff Boone Prescott and his high-handed attitude weren't worth a single tear. Just when she thought she'd gotten a true glimpse of the real Boone Prescott, he'd reared his ugly head and bared his fangs.

Humph! What a joke! He hadn't even listened to what she'd had to say. He'd acted as judge, jury and executioner. What a fool she'd been to think she could ever love a man like him. It had been a ludicrous idea in the first place to even consider settling down with a sheriff who lived in a remote fishing village in Alaska. There wasn't a single shoe retailer in this town that could keep her in the shoe style to which she'd become accustomed.

Not that she'd pinned her hopes and dreams on Boone or anything, but she'd allowed herself to imagine what the future might hold in store for them as a couple. Holding hands as they walked down Jarvis Street. Riding snowmobiles. More ice skating lessons at Deer Run Lake. Against her better judgment, she'd allowed herself to dream of building something lasting with Boone. They'd been foolish dreams! Unrealistic and fanciful. It would take more than a gorgeous sheriff to make her give up the life she'd built for herself in New York.

Humph! It was a moot point. Sheriff Boone Prescott was a cad. It was an expression her mother had always used to describe someone low-down and mean. It was the perfect word to describe the know-it-all sheriff.

Shame on you for taking your eyes off the prize, a little voice buzzed in her ear. Instead of batting her lashes at Boone, she should have been concentrating on the reason she'd traveled over three thousand miles to come to Love. It had been the one thing in her life that didn't make her feel like a failure—her job as a journalist.

Taking a soothing breath, she counted to ten in her head. She needed to calm down before her blood pressure went sky-high. *Focus, Grace.* She reached for her computer, knowing that the only thing to do at this moment to center herself was write. Tony had been pestering her to send him something about life in Love. Well, she was going to write until her fingers cramped up. If Tony wanted a juicy article on this town, then she'd give him one. No holds barred. Before she knew it she'd written the beginnings of an article and the tension she was feeling had eased up some.

Misadventures in Love

There is a woman shortage in Love, Alaska. I've seen it with my own eyes. And despite the male residents' constant speculation as to the whys and wherefores of the situation, it seems pretty straight-forward to this city girl. Male chauvinists. Nean-derthals masquerading as modern-day men. Adult men who brawl over women in cafés. Town sher-iffs who spend their time on coffee breaks instead of keeping law and order in their town.

On and on she went until she felt as if she'd purged herself of all her fury and resentment. It felt good to vent. It felt good to lash out. When she finished the column Grace pressed the send button, feeling a sense of victory rush through her as she watched her article enter cyber-space. Now, she just had one more thing to do before she abandoned this frozen tundra masquerading as a village. She wasn't sticking around this town just to have more abuse heaped on her.

She really didn't belong here in the first place. Hav-ing feelings for the sheriff didn't mean she was going to give up her life in New York to become his Alaskan bride. Sure, she'd thought about what it would be like to settle down here in Love. But giving up her career wasn't something she could easily do. It was an essential part of her identity.

It was just as well that she nipped this whole situa-tion in the bud and headed back home. She had more than enough material to finish the Operation Love series without being planted in the wilds of Alaska.

It wasn't as if she was running away from the situa-tion. Before she booked a one-way flight out of Love, she was going to make a big splash at the emergency town council meeting. According to Hazel they were meeting tonight to discuss the downturn in Love's economy and implement new strategies to stimulate growth.

In a perfect world she would have worn her nude heels with this dress, but given the weather, Hazel's boots made the most sense. She cast a glance in the mirror. Her outfit showed she meant business. She was wearing a dark blazer with her dress and a demure set of pearl earrings. It was the perfect outfit to make a surprise appearance at the town meeting.

Boone Prescott had caught her off guard earlier. He'd mistaken her kindness for weakness and lashed out at her in a completely unacceptable fashion. All she'd been guilty of was trying to be nice to Jasper. He'd misinterpreted everything and called her actions into question. There was a loneliness that hovered around the mayor like a lingering shadow. Although she knew it was tied up with losing the great love of his life, it still struck her as something that should have faded with time. She'd seen the way Hazel looked at Jasper. If only Jasper could see there were still opportunities to love and be loved. It was too bad his sanctimonious grandson didn't seem to care one bit about his quality of life.

Humph! If it was the last thing she did in this rinky-dink town, she was going to give the sheriff of Love a piece of her mind.

"And that, my fellow council members, is my recommendation for our Founder's Day celebration." Dwight Lewis, town treasurer, concluded his report with his usual dramatic flair. He bowed at the waist as if he was greeting royalty.

Boone felt his eyelids growing heavier by the second. He'd been fighting this battle against drowsiness ever since the meeting started an hour ago. Town meetings were duller than the shine on his most scuffed-up pair of cowboy boots.

He couldn't stop thinking about Grace. Blowing up at her had been wrong of him, and he'd been regretting it ever since she'd left without a word. Seeing the look of hurt flash in her eyes had been painful. He'd felt like a bully. For so long he'd considered himself the official head of the Prescott family, the one who protected all the others from harm. He'd lashed out at Grace because of fear. Jasper wasn't getting any younger, and he was terrified of losing him. So many things were up in the air with his loved ones. Grace had been the scapegoat for all his worries.

The things he'd said to her filled him with shame. He didn't like hurting people. Especially Grace. Those quivering lips and wet eyelashes had done a number on him. A part of him wondered if it had been his way of pushing her away a little bit after they'd connected at the skating party and shared that unforgettable kiss. She'd nudged her way into his heart at record speed. And he didn't quite know what to do about all these feelings rumbling around inside him.

How in the world could he make it up to her? He wondered if she liked flowers. No! Shoes. She loved shoes. Maybe he could order a pair from some fancy online shoe vendor.

Boom. A crashing noise jolted him to attention. His eyes flew open at the sight of Grace standing in the doorway with one hand on her hip. Her hat was sitting off to the side, while the tip of her nose was the color of a strawberry. Suddenly, he was wide-awake.

"Miss Corbett," Dwight said in a voice brimming with outrage, "it is highly unorthodox to come crashing into a town meeting."

"I apologize for my interruption, but I came here to say my piece." She tilted her head up. "Don't worry, Dwight. This town won't have to put up with me much longer. I'm ready to head back to New York City as soon as I can make the arrangements." She shook her head and let out a loud harrumph sound. "By the way, I've been sitting out in the hallway waiting for an opportune time to come in. I've never in my life heard such a bunch of baloney wrapped up as good sense. Ever since I came to Love I've heard about all the financial problems and the doom and gloom hovering over this place like a dark cloud."

Dwight shot up from his chair. "Are you just going to sit here and let her insult my report?" Dwight said with a loud sniff of disapproval.

Jasper shook his head. "Sit down, Dwight. You already had the floor." He smiled in Grace's direction. "Continue, Grace. Sorry for the interruption."

Grace cleared her throat. "You have something right under your noses, if only you'd stop feeling sorry for yourselves long enough to notice."

"Mind cluing us in?" Boone drawled.

She didn't want to look at him, but he was practically boring a hole straight through her. And to add insult to injury, he had the nerve to look handsome in his dark jacket and slacks. It would be so much easier to ignore him if he looked like a troll.

She stuck out her foot and pointed. "These boots!"

Jasper's bushy brows knit together. "Books. What about the books?" he asked.

"Boots," Boone leaned toward Jasper and said in a raised voice. "You better start wearing that hearing aid, or you're going to miss out on every conversation in town."

Grace glared at Boone. "If I may be allowed to continue." She swung her gaze toward the other council members, studiously avoiding looking in Boone's direction. "These boots rival some of the biggest names in the business. They're comfortable and well-made and stylish. Trust me. I'm a shoe girl. I know what I'm talking about. I spend way more money than I should on shoes. And I've got quite a few boots in my collection. Cha-ching, if you know what I mean."

"My boots!" Hazel shrieked, a delighted expression etched on her face. "You actually think they're worth something?"

"I think they could be the next big thing," Grace announced. "If only you so-called town leaders would open your eyes and consider the possibilities. When I was lost out in the woods these boots kept me from getting a bad case of hypothermia. They have value!"

"I'm open to anything that will restore this town to her former glory," Jasper said, raising his fist in the air.

Hazel fanned herself with her hand. "And to think that my little boots might help to revitalize our economy. I'm tickled at the prospect."

Grace stretched her arms out wide. "Think of all the ways you could market the boots. The slogan could be 'fashionable and functional.' Customers would eat it up. Not to mention the thrill of buying authentic Alaskan boots."

The dramatic sound of a clearing throat had her turning toward Boone. "It's an amazing idea, Grace. Thoughtful. Pragmatic. And creative. You definitely thought outside the box. I make a motion that we explore the possibility of mass-producing Hazel's boots on a trial run to see if this enterprise has merit." He nodded in Hazel's direction. "With your permission of course, Hazel."

Hazel was grinning so wide she resembled a jack-o'-lantern. "Of course, Boone. You know I'd do anything to help this town."

"You went above and beyond, Grace," Boone said in a silky smooth voice. "Who knows? There might be a spot for you on this town council." He was smiling at her—a beatific smile that almost made her forget his unforgivable behavior from this morning. How could he grin at her after he'd treated her so poorly? Did he think a simple wink and a smile would grant him forgiveness?

"It's a little late for the compliments." She pointed a wavering finger in Boone's direction.

Something in his eyes challenged her bravado, which only served to stoke her anger. "You, Sheriff Prescott, are the most judgmental man I've ever met. You make sweeping assumptions about people without even giving them the opportunity to explain themselves. It must be so nice to always be right about everything and everyone."

She swung her eyes toward Jasper, who had a glimmer in his eye that looked like encouragement. Hazel was hiding a smirk with her hand while a few of the council members were shaking their heads in disapproval.

Dwight stood up and said, "Miss Corbett! This is highly unorthodox. And inappropriate. This session is not open to the public. We follow rules of order here."

Jasper banged his gavel. He shook his finger at Dwight. "Let Grace speak her peace. She's a resident of this town now. And if this beef between the two of them gets squashed, she may become my granddaughter someday."

"Don't count on it!" Grace growled. "I'd rather be single for the rest of my days than end up with someone like your grandson." She shivered dramatically for effect.

"Ouch," Boone said, placing his hand across his chest. "That hurt, Gracie. Can we go outside and talk… privately?"

She folded her arms across her chest and glared at him. "I really have nothing to say to you, Sheriff Prescott. You're just a…meanie!"

A meanie? Had those words really just come out of her mouth? She'd momentarily reverted back to her eight-year-old self. She'd come here to confront Boone and to let the town council know how shortsighted they were being about the town's potential. Now she'd made a fool of herself by spouting juvenile insults. Heat rose to her cheeks as she stomped out of the town meeting. Raucous laughter trailed behind her.

"Of all the stupid, misguided ideas," she muttered to herself.

"Grace!" The sound of Boone calling her name drifted after her as she walked down Jarvis Street. She ignored him, continuing to walk at a fast clip past shops and curious townsfolk.

"Come on, Grace. Please, stop."

She whirled around to find him right on her heels. "What do you want?" she snapped.

She could feel her lips pursing of their own accord. It was a bad habit she'd had ever since childhood.

"I'm a fool. Please don't leave." A tremor danced along his jawline. His eyes blinked rapidly.

Six little words spoken so humbly by Boone nearly did her in. They crashed over her with the weight of a tsunami. It was hard for her to even breathe, let alone speak.

"Why do you want me to stay?" she asked.

"Because you add color to my world. You're like a bright light in the forest. When I'm with you…I laugh more. I feel things I haven't felt in a very long time. You make me believe in things I thought might be behind me. And I lashed out at you…because you're in my thoughts all the time and part of me is scared of what I feel for you. It was my way, I think, of pushing you away. The thing is, I want you in my life, Gracie. I care so very much about you."

Tears pooled in Grace's eyes. Boone's words traveled all the way to the depths of her soul. No man had ever laid it on the line like this before, not even her ex-fiancé. No one had ever told her what she brought into their world. She'd never imagined her heart could expand to three times its normal size. Emotion clogged her throat, and she was afraid to speak for fear she might blubber like a baby.

A muscle was twitching by Boone's mouth. He looked as if he was about to jump out of his skin. "Grace, say something. Anything. Please."

"You had me at 'I'm a fool,'" Grace said, watching as Boone's body language instantly changed.

Boone easily swallowed up the distance between them. He placed his hands around her waist and dipped her backward before planting a kiss on her lips. His arm was bracing her lower back. Grace rested her hands on his shoulders, surprised and delighted at the unexpected kiss. As his lips moved over hers, Grace couldn't help but think it was the most romantic moment of her life.

He was literally sweeping her off her feet. The sound of clapping interrupted the moment. Boone swung her up so she was standing. The entire town council, minus Dwight, stood a few feet away, their faces lit up with interest and approval. Grace blushed as Boone reached for her hand and raised it to his lips, causing even more of a reaction from the crowd.

This was happiness! Less than an hour ago she'd been angry and distraught and teary.

And in a moment of weakness she'd written a very unflattering article about Love that might get published if she didn't retract it, which she planned to do immediately. Her stomach muscles clenched at the mere thought of the article being published. It had been a petty and small thing to do. It was amazing how quickly things changed.

Now she was practically floating on air. All because of a few humble, sincere words from Boone. Mood swings. Going from jubilation to despair to joy again. Wanting to stay in Love, then wanting to head back to New York City the very next minute. White noise began to thrum in her ears as she began to connect the dots.

This thing between her and Boone was more than a mere flirtation. For Grace, it was beginning to feel a lot like love. And for the life of her, she wasn't sure how she felt about falling for the sheriff.

Chapter Eleven

Boone had known he was a goner the minute Grace had come barreling into the town council meeting last night with guns blazing. From the moment she'd appeared, he'd been forced to stifle the urge to sweep her up in his arms and kiss her senseless. The joy he'd felt when she'd accepted his apology had been indescribable. It was as if, suddenly, all was right with the world.

He couldn't escape the feeling that God was trying to tell him something. Despite her head-turning looks, Grace Corbett was not the type of woman he would ever have imagined as his soul mate. He'd judged her by her love of high heels and her city-girl background. He'd tried to convince himself that a woman like Grace would want the world offered to her on a silver platter. So far, he'd been as wrong about her as a man could be.

Judge not, lest ye be judged.

It wasn't right to judge someone based on initial impressions or superficial things such as the type of shoes they wore. What if Grace had viewed him as nothing more than a backwoods lawman? Their relationship would never have gotten off the ground if that were the case.

Yes, indeed. God was moving his heart in a direction he would never have predicted. One never knew how God might light a path. For a long time he'd been stumbling around in the darkness.

A gentle knocking on his office door drew him out of his thoughts. He was so used to visitors crashing uninvited into his office that the idea of someone using their social graces surprised him.

"Come on in," he called out.

The first thing he saw peeking around the door frame was a head of beautiful raven-colored hair. Grace's pretty face came into view, instantly transforming this ho-hum day into a special one.

"Hey, Gracie. To what do I owe this visit?" Grace advanced toward him, her petite figure decked out in a pink dress that skimmed her knees. She wore a black ski jacket, Hazel's boots and a cute little pink hat on her head. He might be biased, but he thought she was the most adorable woman on the planet.

"Hi, Boone. Sorry for just popping in like this." Her gaze swung around the room as she looked around his office with obvious interest. Kona perked up her ears and sauntered over to Grace at a fast clip. She immediately began lavishing Grace with her undivided attention. Boone smiled at the enthusiastic way Grace embraced Kona. Little by little Grace was showing him that despite first impressions, she fit seamlessly into every single aspect of his life. It reinforced every single notion he'd always heard about finding that one special person. Everything just felt right.

He stood up from his chair and quickly made his way

toward her. "Don't be sorry. This is the highlight of my day." He reached out and pulled her toward him, brushing a swift kiss across her lips. He leaned back on his desk and pulled her closer toward him.

She met his gaze head-on. Her eyes radiated concern. "I need to talk to you about something. It's a little bit delicate."

"C'mon, Gracie. You can tell me anything." And he meant it. He wanted Grace to be able to share anything with him that was weighing on her heart. Judging by the expression on her face, she was torn up about something.

Grace bit her lip. "It's about Jasper's legend."

He stifled the desire to sigh. "I thought we put all this to rest," Boone said, reminding himself that he didn't want to lose his temper with Grace. Not when they'd just gotten over a bumpy patch in the road.

"It's not what you think, Boone. The other day when I was at the mayor's office there was something bothering me about Jasper's timeline."

Boone drew his eyebrows together. "Timeline? What timeline?"

"Jasper has a timeline showing when your ancestor Bodine Prescott discovered gold in Juneau. It shows his untimely death, as well. But there's a problem with it."

"A problem?" Boone asked. "What's the problem?"

Grace heaved a tremendous sigh. "I did a little research, and Jasper's timeline is all wrong. According to the official records related to the Juneau Gold Rush and death records for the state of Alaska, Bodine Prescott passed away in 1879, six months or so before gold was discovered in that area."

The discovery hit him hard. He frowned. "So, you're saying that there never was any treasure."

Grace shook her head, her expression morose. "It seems unlikely that he could have discovered gold in Juneau prior to the documented first discoveries in that area. And there's something else!" She opened up an envelope and pulled out a sheet of paper. She moved closer to him and pointed at a spot on the page. "I found this, too. It's a record of a steamboat sinking out on Kachemak Bay. There were ninety men on board, most of whom perished. Read this part."

Boone took the paper and read the sentence Grace was pointing at. "The men were traveling to Juneau, Alaska, in the hopes of joining a gold expedition led by Joe Juneau."

Boone didn't know how to explain the feelings roaring through him. Even though he'd grown to resent talk of the town legend involving his ancestor, it felt disappointing to discover it had all been nothing more than a tall tale passed on from generation to generation. That knowledge would be devastating to Jasper, who believed in it with all his heart and soul.

"I think it's only right to tell him," Grace said, voicing the exact thing he was thinking. Although it would crush his grandfather to know he'd been chasing fool's gold, it would be kinder in the long run. Lies, whether little white ones or the bold-faced variety, always backfired in the end. He bowed his head, saying a silent prayer for wisdom.

"I'd like for the two of us to tell him together," Grace said in a soft voice.

"Me, too," Boone said. "Honestly, I'm a little nervous about his reaction. I can't imagine what it would be like to have to stop believing in something that's sustained you for a lifetime."

Grace quirked her mouth. "Well then, I guess you're talking to the right person. I've been struggling with my faith for a while now. It's so hard for me to believe in God when it felt like He didn't hear any of my prayers."

"Did you ever stop to thank God for all your blessings?"

Grace frowned. She shook her head. "No, I didn't. I praised Him at times, but I never stopped to thank Him for all the good things that came my way."

Boone reached out and caressed the side of Grace's cheek. It felt as soft as butter. "So how can you blame Him for every heartache and disappointment? If you aren't lifting Him up in praise for the blessings, how can you turn your back on him with every setback?"

Boone was hoping his matter-of-fact statement would settle around Grace like the warm boots encasing her feet. He wanted her to know, in no uncertain terms, that God hadn't punished her when her marriage plans had fallen apart and her family treated her so poorly. And even if it seemed as if He hadn't been listening to her prayers, God would never forsake her.

She nodded as a look of calm passed over her face. "I'm beginning to understand that. Being here in Love has helped me realize that we all go through hard times. No one is immune to it. Jasper. Liam. Honor. And you, too, Boone. It doesn't mean He doesn't love me. And it doesn't even mean He didn't answer my prayers. It just wasn't in the way I wanted at that moment. I need to open my heart to realize where God is leading me. Maybe then I'll know what prayer He answered."

Boone reached out and cupped her chin in his hand. "He's led you here for a reason. Maybe one of those reasons is to shine a light on this legend business and to serve as an instrument for Jasper coming to terms with the truth. He needs you, Gracie." His fingers reached up and gently traced the outline of her full ruby lips. "I need you."

Grace's sweet lips curved upward into a smile. "It's nice to hear that." She reached out and laced her fingers with his. "And I need you, too, Boone. More and more every day." It was a scary thought, since their worlds were night and day. She was a city girl, through and through, while there was no doubt about Boone being a rugged lawman. Although she was falling in love with this town, her heart still belonged to New York City and her job at the *Tribune*. Boone would be as out of place in the Big Apple as a snowman on a tropical island. It would be painful for either one of them to have to choose.

"So, Gracie, how are we going to break the news to Jasper?"

A dinner date at Boone's house should have filled Grace with a feeling of anticipation, but as she worked the afternoon shift at the café, all she could do was fret. Boone had invited Jasper to dinner with them so they could talk to him about everything she'd discovered with her research. Over and over again in her head she practiced the words she would use to break Jasper's heart.

"Why don't you take a break, Grace? You haven't even stopped for a bite to eat," Sophie said as she walked into the kitchen.

"I'm not hungry, Sophie," she murmured. There were too many butterflies flying around her stomach to leave any room for food. All she'd been doing was offering up prayers for wisdom and discernment.

"A cup of coffee might be the perfect pick-me-up."

Sophie flashed a brilliant smile at her. "There's love in the bottom of every cup."

There's love in the bottom of every cup. It was the slogan for Java Giant, the huge coffee chain she'd worked at four years ago. In the two weeks she'd worked there, a giant-sized picture of the owner's daughter had greeted her every morning. The smiling, red-haired girl was the poster girl for the company. Over the years she'd become their brand. It was Sophie! Now she knew why Sophie had always seemed so familiar to her.

"Y-you!" Grace said, pointing at Sophie. She took a step backward. "You're her. Java Giant. You're—"

Sophie's face crumpled. "Grace, please. I can explain everything."

"No! No! Please! I don't want to hear it," Grace said in a raised voice, vehemently shaking her head from side to side. "I don't want to know what a billionaire's daughter is doing in Love, Alaska, working at a café your father could buy and sell a million times over. I don't want to know why you ditched the Mattson name, either."

Sophie took a step toward her. "You're my friend. I want you to know why I'm here. And why I'm going by Miller instead of Mattson. It's been so hard sitting on this secret. My family's business is not who I am. I was so tired of people wanting to be around me because of my father and the family fortune. Everyone in my life wanted something from me, usually money or a high-profile job with my father's corporation. A man even pretended to love me just so he could marry the Java Giant heiress. I just became so hurt by it all that I wanted to go somewhere and be anonymous so I can find love."

"And you don't want anyone here to know who you really are?" Grace asked.

"They can't know, Grace. Take it from me. People start treating me differently when they find out about the Java Giant connection. I've been dealing with it my whole life." Tears began gathering in Sophie's eyes. Grace reached out and clutched her friend's hand, wishing she could take away Sophie's pain.

Although Grace didn't completely understand Sophie's situation or what exactly had led her to hide out in Love, she knew enough about her to know that she was a woman of faith and conviction. She also knew firsthand the pressures in keeping secrets in this type of atmosphere. Love was a tight-knit, small town where newcomers were welcomed with warmth and generosity. It didn't feel right to lie to them. It led to guilt and fear and shame. She felt all those things. On some level she knew Sophie must be struggling with those issues, as well.

And Grace didn't want to be in a position to betray Sophie the way she was betraying every single resident of this town she'd grown to love. There was no doubt in her mind that a story about the Java Giant heiress living in a remote fishing village would be a major coup for the *Tribune*. Tony would salivate at the prospect of getting his hands on a story like that.

"There are people who've been hired to find me. I know how my daddy operates. But I trust you not to tell anyone," Sophie said tearfully.

"You shouldn't. I am not a trustworthy person," she said fiercely.

Sophie's eyes bulged. "But of course you are. You're one of the finest people I've ever known." Sophie wrapped her arms around her in an embrace of friendship and solidarity. Grace clung to her friend like a life preserver. She now knew she would never betray Sophie.

It just wasn't possible. This woman had kindness and warmth and an almost childlike innocence that Grace refused to exploit. She may have compromised her morals by going undercover in Love, but she wasn't going to compound her mistakes by revealing Sophie's secret.

Somehow that knowledge gave her hope. Maybe she wasn't as bad a person as she believed herself to be. Maybe she could turn this whole thing around and tell Boone the truth before the articles came out. She'd emailed Tony and left a few messages about withdrawing her snarky article about Love. He'd sent her a message telling her not to worry about it and to keep sending more articles his way.

What if she wrote a hopeful article about Love? One that focused on the hardworking townsfolk and the attempts to revitalize the town. She could focus on the popularity of the Moose Café and the successful fishermen who'd been providing fish as export for generations. And if she wrote about Hazel's boots, perhaps it could create a little buzz about them. Maybe that way it wouldn't sting so badly when the truth came out.

"Your secret is safe with me. It isn't mine to tell," Grace said.

"Thank you, Grace," Sophie said, closing her eyes as she let out a sigh of relief.

"What's all the ruckus back here?" Hazel poked her head in the kitchen door. "We need someone to make some frappés."

"I'll do it," Grace volunteered, surprising herself by speaking up. Even though she was far from an expert, she was learning the ropes at the café and serving up tasty drinks that more times than not earned her compliments from the customers. Despite the daily challenges, she liked working at the Moose Café. Most of all she liked being part of a community. She enjoyed serving the customers and having conversations with them about everything under the sun.

Day by day she was settling more and more into the fabric of this town. Every moment she spent in Boone's presence only served to heighten her feelings for him. And even though it gave her a sense of peace it also scared her a little bit, because she had no idea how she was going to untangle herself from all the lies she'd told since arriving in Love.

That evening she borrowed Hazel's truck and carefully navigated the snow-packed roads to Boone's rustic stone-and-cedar home nestled in the wooded area near Deer Run Lake. She was proud of herself for tackling the driving issue head-on. It was yet another thing to check off her list.

Boone, dressed in jeans and a cream sweater, opened the door with Kona at his side. Her insides did flip-flops at the sight of him. His sandy hair looked a little rumpled, as if he'd just awoken from a nap. She resisted the impulse to reach out and smooth it down.

"Come on in, Gracie. You look beautiful."

His compliment swept over her like a gentle breeze. She'd grown up in a household where it was considered vain to focus on looks. Her parents had never even told her she was pretty. Nothing felt better than to hear it from Boone's lips.

"Your home is lovely," Grace said, admiring the gleaming pine floors and the elaborate stone fireplace.

He gestured her to follow him down the hall. "I've got something on the stove."

When she entered his light and airy kitchen, a tangy smell rose to her nostrils. Her stomach rumbled in appreciation. She looked over at Boone. He was at the stove stirring a pot of chili. A pan of corn bread sat on the stove right next to a covered dish. A big bowl of salad sat on the butcher block counter.

"You made all this?" she asked. She could hear the surprise ringing out in her voice.

"Of course I did," he said with a laugh. "I love to cook."

Score! A man who enjoyed cooking. Yet again, Boone was surprising her. What was next? Was he going to start reciting Shakespearean sonnets or drawing masterpieces? So far, he'd demonstrated he was a man of many talents.

"Can I do anything?" she asked as she took in the cozy kitchen. Copper pots hung from a rack, white and gray tiles accented the space behind his stove and the hardwood floors gleamed. It was the type of kitchen she could imagine herself cooking meals for a family in. A room where she and Boone might cook a meal together as they listened to romantic music on the radio or recounted the events of their day to one another. Hmm. How had her thoughts wandered so easily toward a shared future?

"If you wouldn't mind setting the table, that would be great." Boone threw out the suggestion and Grace immediately began laying out the plates and cutlery for three people.

The sound of halting footsteps heralded Jasper's arrival. He showed up in the doorway leaning on his crutches, just as Boone was putting the finishing touches on his chili. Within minutes they were all seated at the table, with Boone saying the blessing. "Lord, bless this food for the nourishment of our bodies and our souls.

I'm very thankful to be sharing a meal with two very special people. Thank You, Lord, for all our blessings."

They ate in companionable silence. A few times Jasper stopped to praise Boone's cooking. Grace was impressed. No man had ever cooked a meal for her like this one.

Finally, Jasper placed his fork down on the table and wiped his mouth with his napkin. His eyes were trained on Boone. "So, what's this all about? I know you didn't invite me here for my good looks."

Grace looked over at Boone, who gave her a slight nod of encouragement.

"There's something we'd like to talk to you about. Something important," Grace hedged. She bit the inside of her lip, unsure how to proceed. Since Boone had always discouraged Jasper in his pursuit of the family treasure, he thought Grace should be the one to break the bad news. That way, Jasper wouldn't suspect his grandson was simply trying to discourage him in his pursuits.

"Wait a minute!" Jasper cried out. "Is this an engagement announcement?"

Boone rolled his eyes. "No, Jasper. This has nothing to do with Gracie and me."

"Humph! Okay. If you say so," Jasper grumbled. "Would have been nice to say my grandson was the first person who made it down the aisle under Operation Love."

Boone none too subtly jabbed his grandfather with his elbow. Grace didn't miss the warning look he sent in his grandfather's direction. If she wasn't dreading telling Jasper what her research had revealed, she might have laughed at the dynamic between the two men.

"Can't blame me for hoping," Jasper muttered.

Hope. Jasper was a man who lived every day of his life

with hope in his heart. It was the reason she was dreading this conversation. She prayed this information would provide discernment.

Grace ducked her head down and fumbled with her napkin. She felt as if a huge weight was sitting on her shoulders. This sweet, sentimental man was her friend and she didn't want to crush him. Still she owed him the truth. "Jasper, I need to tell you something about the treasure."

Jasper rubbed his hands together. "Don't be shy. You know I love to talk treasure."

"Well, this might not be the type of conversation you're anticipating," Boone warned.

Jasper looked back and forth between them, his expression wary.

"I looked at some online archives related to the Juneau Gold Rush," Grace spit out. "The dates don't match up. Bodine Prescott didn't find gold in Juneau, Jasper." She shook her head, feeling mournful. "It's not possible since he drowned months before the first prospectors struck gold."

"No, that can't be right," Jasper said in a raised voice. "That doesn't make any sense."

Boone leaned in and placed his hand on Jasper's shoulder. "Gracie checked and double-checked. She looked at the archives. There's a list of the men who found gold in Juneau. They had to register their claims. There's nothing listed under Bodine Prescott."

"Jasper, I think when Bodine and his brother went on that steamship they were trying to join an expedition in Juneau. I found some records to support that idea. He didn't discover gold, but I think he was an adventurer who was eager to make history and help his family gain financial independence. He died in that pursuit."

She got up and began to dig through her purse. She found the papers she was looking for and handed them to Jasper. Boone and Grace watched as Jasper began reading the document about the steamship tragedy and the men who'd been on their way to the adventure of a lifetime in Juneau. There was also a copy of Bodine's death record. Jasper let out a sigh and rubbed his eyes. He didn't say a word.

Tears filled her eyes. Even though they were doing the right thing by connecting the dots for Jasper, they were snatching away his dream, one he'd been chasing since he was a little boy.

Not able to stand the silence anymore, Grace spoke. "I'm really sorry about the treasure. I want you to know, I really hoped you'd find it."

He patted her hand. "I know you did, sweetheart. And there's no need to be sorry. Sometimes life throws us curveballs. It's been a diversion, an opportunity to dream for a little while and escape my troubles."

Jasper's response surprised her. "But aren't you disappointed? You've spent most of your life believing in it and looking for it."

"True. But when it comes down to it, I've gained more than I lost. I was chasing something elusive. The love of my family, your friendship, Hazel, the fellowship of the residents of this town…that's real. I can reach out and touch those things. My relationship with God is real."

"You're handling this really well, Grandpa. Is there anything we can do to help?" Boone asked.

"Aww. I love it when you call me Grandpa." Jasper looked at his grandson, his eyes twinkling with mischief.

"Well, if you really want to help me, you'll get married and make me a great-grandfather again so little Aidan can have a playmate."

"Jasper!" Boone growled.

Grace looked back and forth between the two men. A giggle rose up inside her and burst forth, emerging as a hybrid of a snort and a chuckle. She covered her mouth with her hand and despite her best efforts, couldn't contain her laughter. Jasper had been dealt a blow tonight, and he'd handled it with grace and aplomb. Rather than wallowing in self-pity, Jasper was being his usual playful self and teasing Boone. Jasper met her gaze and winked at her.

This was home, she thought. A place where you felt comfortable in your own skin no matter what was being laid on the table. Being able to turn sorrow into laughter and emerge all the stronger for the hardships that came your way. After a lifetime of wanting to be accepted, Grace knew she was firmly rooted in her nesting place. She loved New York City and all its wonders, but she chose Love, Alaska, and the sheriff who'd made a believer out of her. This was the home she'd always wanted. Right here with the man she'd fallen in love with. This was where she wanted her future to unfold, right here in Love. But with all the lies that were standing between her and Boone, she had no idea how she was going to find the courage to tell him the truth. Would he turn away from her if he knew?

Chapter Twelve

In the weeks and days after Grace's discovery about the legend of Bodine Prescott, Boone grew a new measure of respect for his grandfather. Jasper didn't wallow in the news or try to bury his head in the sand about the facts Grace had presented. He dealt with it with grace, charm and a good measure of humor. Watching the way he handled himself showed Boone a lot about humility and wisdom.

Rather than dwelling on anything he'd lost, Jasper had decided to focus on Grace's idea about Hazel's boots. Tonight's town council meeting would be held at the Moose Café in order for the townsfolk to weigh in on the proposed plans to start mass-producing the boots and creating a corporation to oversee it. There was a lot of buzz surrounding the meeting and a sense of excitement and anticipation pulsed in the air.

By the time Boone arrived at the meeting, it was standing room only. Grace, wearing a fuzzy pink sweater and a matching skirt, stood up from across the room and waved at him. She pointed to the seat next to hers and motioned him over. Curious eyes swung in their direction, but he shrugged off the attention. Pretty soon the whole town would be buzzing about Sheriff Prescott and the beautiful barista.

"I saved it for you," she said as soon as he reached her side, removing the coat resting on the seat.

"Thanks. This place is packed," he said, feeling a sense of contentment about Grace saving a spot for him. It was little things like this that warmed his heart almost to the point of overflowing. It was a new feeling for him. And sometimes he just wanted to shout it out from the rooftops.

"I'm not sure I know what to say," Grace whispered. A nervous tremor danced alongside her jaw. She fiddled with her fingers.

Boone put his arm around her. "Say exactly what you said at the last town council meeting. With the same amount of passion and conviction. You'll have them eating out of your hands."

Grace smiled at him. She began to relax right before his eyes. "Thanks for the pep talk. I just want everyone in town to realize that the boots are a great investment with wonderful potential for growth," Grace said in a determined voice.

Boone chuckled. "Sounds like you have your presentation all figured out."

Within minutes Jasper called the meeting to order. Boone quickly scanned the room. He nodded in the direction of a few people who made eye contact. Cameron waved at him and shook his head at the large crowd. Hank Jeffries was seated front and center, no doubt in the hopes of catching a glimpse of Grace. Gunther and Wanda held hands at a table. It seemed everyone's curiosity had been piqued by the topic of tonight's meeting.

"Welcome, everyone. This meeting has been called tonight to put forth an idea presented by Grace Corbett, a wonderful young woman who has recently moved to Love. She came to us with this terrific idea about mass-producing Hazel's boots. It has the potential to create a solid economy in Love. Why don't I call her up here so she can explain it to you? She's much nicer to look at than I am," he said with a chuckle.

Laughter rose up in the room. Grace ran her hands over her skirt and smoothed it down. After darting a quick look in Boone's direction, she rose from her seat and took center stage next to Jasper.

Boone didn't know why, but his palms began to moisten with nervousness. He so wanted Grace to do well. And he was fully prepared to intervene if anyone gave her a hard time.

"Good evening, everyone. I'm Grace. Grace Corbett," she said with a slight nod of her head. A loud chorus of good evenings rang out in the café. "Even though I'm a newcomer to Love, I've found myself caring very deeply about this town. I want it to thrive. Ever since I arrived in town I've heard about some financial setbacks the town has been experiencing. That's happening to a lot of communities around this country. But what this town has, in my humble opinion, is something that a lot of towns don't have. Heart. Pluck. Resilience. Fellowship. And because of all those things, I think if this entire town stands behind Hazel's boots and chips in to make them a red-hot commodity, they could really help this town make it through this downturn. There are so many ways to help. Promotion. Man power. Seed money. Let's stand together and give it our all."

People stood up and cheered as soon as Grace stopped

talking. Boone was among them. Jasper beamed with pride. Hazel put two fingers together and let out a loud whistle. Grace's face lit up with joy.

The door to the café burst open with a bang. A disheveled-looking Dwight stood in the doorway, a fierce expression etched on his face. He clutched a folder to his chest.

"Quiet, Dwight. Grace is in the middle of a presentation," someone called out to him.

Dwight squeezed his way through the crowd and made his way to the front. "Grace Corbett is not who you think she is," he announced in a loud voice. He paused for a moment to adjust his glasses. "She is masquerading as a participant in Operation Love when in reality she is a journalist. Frankly, she's nothing more than a fraud."

A shocked silence filled the room, right before a buzz began to thrum among the townsfolk.

"That's ridiculous, Dwight," Boone said, moving toward the front so he could stand next to Grace.

"Actually it's not," Dwight said. "Read it and weep." Dwight shoved a piece of paper at Boone.

Grace felt paralyzed. She couldn't move. Couldn't speak. And she had no idea what Dwight was showing Boone. All she knew was that her world was on the verge of collapse.

"What is this?" Boone asked, his brows knitted together.

Dwight turned toward her and asked, "Would you like to do the honors, Miss Corbett? Or should I?"

Although Grace wanted to do something about the smug expression on Dwight's face, she felt a desperate need to know what Boone held in his hands. How could she explain when she had no clue what was going on?

"It's an article written by Grace Corbett for the *New York Tribune*. It just went viral, and it's about us…and this town," Dwight explained. He shot her a scornful look. "Tsk. Tsk. You said some very mean-spirited things about us."

Article? What article? Mean-spirited? Tony had promised her that he wouldn't be posting any of the articles until she was back home in New York City. How could this be happening?

Panic grabbed her by the throat. She needed to talk to Boone in private. Grace tugged at Boone's sleeve. "I need to talk to you. In private."

Boone was reading the piece of paper. His eyes were scanning it with single-minded focus. He swung his gaze toward her. All the light had been extinguished from his eyes. His expression was shuttered.

"Gracie, say something. Tell him it's a big misunderstanding." His tone was flat, as if he didn't even believe what he was saying.

A huge lump had formed in her throat. "I can't Boone. I wish I could, but I can't."

The look of puzzlement etched on his face was replaced by one of comprehension. "You wrote this… hatchet piece?" He ran a hand over his face. "Neanderthals masquerading as modern-day men. Is that your handiwork?"

Grace felt all the color drain from her face. Wait a minute. How in the world had her snarky article been printed for all the world to see? She'd withdrawn it. Tony had agreed that it would never see the light of day. It was a moot point now. The wild bucking bronco had been let out of the stable, and she had to deal with the fallout.

She chewed on her thumbnail. "I know it looks bad, Boone—"

"Bad?" Boone scoffed. "This is so far past bad I can't see straight."

People were talking loudly in the background, but at the moment all she cared about was Boone. She needed him to understand. "I'm sorry for not being honest with you."

"So you came here as a journalist looking for a story?" Boone asked, his tone incredulous.

"Yes, Boone. I did. I'm a journalist for a newspaper in New York. And the reason I came here was to write a story about the town and Operation Love. The only way I can explain it is to tell you that for a very long time my job has been the only constant thing in my life."

Gasps rang out in the café. Loud whispers reached her ears. Her gaze never strayed from Boone.

"So, you didn't come here looking for love?" Boone's voice cracked with emotion.

Tears stung her eyes, but she refused to cry. She'd done this. Every bit of it. And if nothing else, she needed to own it. "No, Boone. I didn't come to Alaska looking for love." *But I found it anyway. With you.* The words stuck in her throat.

Upon making her stark confession, Grace felt as if the ground underneath her was shifting. Suddenly, her world was tilting wildly on its axis. She needed fresh air, because at the moment she couldn't seem to catch a breath. The pain she felt was a thousand times worse than anything she'd ever known. Boone grasped her by the arm and pulled her to the front door of the Moose Café, moving past the throng of townsfolk. Once they were outside he released her arm and moved a few steps away from her, as if he didn't even want to be near her.

He shoved his hand through his hair. With eyes flashing fire, he locked gazes with her. "One question. Did you write those words?" he asked.

Grace nodded. For a person who'd always had an ability with words, right now she had none at her disposal. She looked down, unable to meet Boone's unforgiving stare.

"There's nothing real about you. You're a sham. An absolute and utter fake." He ground the words out as if they were poison.

"The way I feel about you is one-hundred percent real," she said in a quiet voice.

Boone scoffed. "If you think I believe that, Grace Corbett, I have a cannery to sell you."

"Can we sit down somewhere quiet and talk this over? Maybe if we—" she said.

"There is no *we*. Not after what I just read. Not after what you just admitted. To tell you the honest truth, I never want to see you again." With one last, scathing look, Boone turned on his heel and began walking away from her.

Grace watched Boone walk away from her without making a single attempt at convincing him to stay. There had been something in his tone and the look in his eyes that spoke volumes. It was over. All her hopes and dreams for building something lasting with Boone had crashed and burned. Just when she'd had everything she'd ever wanted in the palm of her hand, it had all blown up in her face. And she couldn't help but think she deserved every ounce of Boone's scorn.

* * *

Walking back into the Moose Café was one of the most difficult things she'd ever done in her life. Strangely enough, it was way worse than explaining to a church full of guests that her wedding had been called off. Shame coursed through her as she pushed the door open and crossed the threshold. A roomful of people stared at her with censure in their eyes. She scanned the room looking for Jasper. Kind, sweet Jasper, who'd taught her so much about pluck and grit in the past few weeks. He was standing with Hazel at the sit-down counter. He shook his head at her in disbelief, his eyes filled with pain. Hazel simply stared at her, her expression shuttered. Cameron crossed his arms across his chest and studied her from across the room. Sophie sent her an encouraging smile.

She walked toward the front of the room and stood in the same spot she'd been standing when she'd addressed the crowd earlier about Hazel's boots. This time there was no question about her trembling limbs. She felt as if she was facing a firing squad. Nervously, she cleared her throat. "I'm not here to make excuses. Frankly, there aren't any. I came to Love under false pretenses. I came here to write about Operation Love and the people in this town." Tears were streaming down her face now and she didn't bother to wipe them away. Her heart had shattered into a million pieces. She had nothing left to lose. "I wrote a bunch of articles. Only one of them was nasty. I wrote it because I was upset with Boone and I lashed out in the only way I knew how. Right afterward I withdrew it, and my editor promised not to publish it. That's the truth.

"For a long time now my job as a journalist has been everything to me. It was my identity. So when the opportunity came up to write a series about Love, I jumped at it. I never imagined that I would fall for this town. I had no idea I'd be torn between going back to New York City and staying here. By lying to everyone in town, I abused the trust you placed in me. You let me into your lives…and your hearts. I betrayed your belief in me. I can't tell you how sorry I am about that. Because I love this town. You've shown me more grace and acceptance than my own family ever has. And I'll never forget any of you. Truly, I won't."

She swung her gaze toward Jasper and Hazel. "Jasper. Please forgive me. Your loyalty to this town is a thing of beauty. You've inspired me in every way possible. And Hazel, you've opened up your home to me and been my friend. Please don't let my actions take away from the town's plans for your boots. They are brilliant." She turned toward Cameron. "Thanks for hiring me, Cameron. Working at the Moose Café made me feel like I belonged in this town. I've never felt that sense of belonging before. Because of all of you I'd made the decision to stay here in Love, even though I know now I can't."

And it hurt so badly to know she no longer had a place here, because she'd never had a home before. Not even in New York City or at the *Tribune*. Of course that knowledge would sweep over her just as she was being run out of town on a rail. Before she completely broke down she looked over at Sophie, who was dabbing at her eyes with a tissue. "Thanks for your friendship, Sophie. It breaks my heart that I let you down."

"What about the sheriff?" someone called out.

"He hates me," she choked out. "And I don't blame him one single bit."

Grace stumbled through the crowd in a haze of tears

until she wound up outside in the bitter cold. She deeply inhaled the Alaskan air, savoring the crisp, pristine feel of it as it seared her lungs. This time tomorrow Alaska would be nothing more than a memory. She would try with all her might to remember every little detail of this charming town. She pressed her eyes closed in an attempt to capture all of Love's unique aspects in her mind's eye. However, all she could see was Boone's ruggedly hand-some face and the look of utter devastation on it when he'd discovered the truth.

Chapter Thirteen

The following morning, Boone dragged himself over to the Moose Café for breakfast. There were about a dozen customers already sitting at tables. Some studiously avoided his gaze while others went out of their way to come over to his table to greet him. Cameron had called him late the night before to tell him that Grace had quit her barista job, so he knew he wasn't going to be running into her at the Moose Café. Although every instinct had urged him to stay at home today and wallow in his misery, he was determined to prove a point. Grace's betrayal hadn't broken him. He was still standing. And he wanted everyone in the café to see it and pass it on to whomever they came across in their travels. No doubt everyone in town would be comparing this incident to the day he'd found out about Diana's betrayal with another man.

There was really no comparison. What he felt for Grace was ten times as powerful as what he'd felt for his ex-girlfriend. Being made a laughingstock by Grace was a wound he didn't think he would recover from. Not in this lifetime.

He was in love with Grace. Deeply, profoundly in love with her. Which is why he was sitting at this table at her former place of employment, toying with the idea of forgiving her and begging her to stay. The very idea of it made him feel like a major league sucker.

Neanderthals masquerading as modern-day men.

Each and every time he thought about forgiving Grace, the words from the article came into sharp focus. *Town sheriffs who spend their time on coffee breaks instead of keeping law and order in their town.*

"What are you doing? Drowning your sorrows in cappuccino?" Declan's voice intruded on his thoughts.

Boone had an urge to swing his feet up on the empty chair and deny his best friend a seat. He had the feeling Declan had come to the Moose Café armed with words of wisdom. Before he could act on his impulse, Declan slid into the seat, placed his elbows on the table and stared him down.

Boone lowered his gaze to his steaming mug and took a sip. "What makes you think I'm hurting?"

Declan shook his head, his expression mutinous. "Come on. You can pull that 'I'm doing fine—how's the weather?' routine with everyone else in this town. But it doesn't work with me, okay? That look on your face—some might call it a hangdog expression. Others might say you had your heart handed to you on a platter."

He opened his mouth to object, but a golf ball–sized lump sat lodged in his throat. What was the point in denying it to Declan? He'd see right through his facade.

"You'd think I would've learned my lesson last go-round. Grace played me for a chump. She played all of us."

Blue eyes pierced right through him. "Life is rarely as simple as you're trying to make it."

"Don't, Declan. I don't think I can stomach your taking up for her." Boone bowed his head as pain crashed over him.

"Boone, what I've seen in the past few weeks is something I thought I'd never see again. You've been joyful. You laugh more. And you ditched that chip on your shoulder. I figure Grace must have knocked it off. You two are great together. She's changed you, in every way possible a person can be transformed. That's real."

Boone shook his head, resisting his best friend's sentiments. "She wasn't real. All she did was pretend to be somebody we'd all fall in love with so she could get a story."

"Who are you trying to convince?" Cameron's voice came from behind him. "The rest of us? Or yourself?"

"I should have known better than to come in here today," Boone grumbled as Cameron moved into his line of vision.

"That woman has changed this town. And she's not the same lady who fell into your arms on the dock. She's strong. And creative. And kind. And if someone's in trouble, she's there, wanting to help." Cameron threw his hands in the air. "And if you can't see that…maybe you don't deserve her, Sheriff."

Boone jumped up from his chair, causing the frothy cup of cappuccino to spill onto the table. "Don't you get it?" he ground out. "She's just like Diana. She lied to me." He swung his gaze from Cameron to Declan. "How did I get to be the one in the wrong?"

"Diana?" a loud voice barked behind him. He spun around, coming face-to-face with his grandfather.

Just perfect! Jasper had arrived just in time to join forces with Cameron and Declan. Suddenly everyone was coming out of the woodwork to gang up on him. Meanwhile, Grace was probably holed up in her cabin licking her wounds while he was taking all the hits.

Jasper snorted. "She's nothing like Diana. She's got more heart and soul in her little pinky than that one had in her whole body. You're a stubborn fool, Boone. After you took off last night she begged the town for forgiveness. It was one of the most moving things I've ever seen. Humph! Serves you right she's gone and left Love."

Boone frowned at Jasper. What was he babbling about? Who'd gone where?

"Left?" he asked, his tone raspy. "What are you talking about?" His mouth felt as dry as a desert. Feeling unsettled, he sank back down into his seat.

"She left first thing this morning on a seven-thirty plane. I heard a charter outfit from Homer picked her up. That will get her into Anchorage by eight thirty or so. Then she'll be heading back to the Big Apple," Jasper explained, a frustrated expression etched on his face.

"S-she's gone?" Boone tripped over the words as the harsh reality settled over him.

Jasper snorted. "Congrats, grandson. You got your wish. Grace Corbett is out of your life for good." Jasper's eyes were as bleak as the Alaskan tundra.

He felt the heat of a dozen pairs of eyes on him. Many were filled with anger, while others seemed to pity him.

Hazel sniffed back tears. "Grace is one of a kind. She opened my eyes to things. I'm so tired of love being tossed aside because of pride and misunderstandings. I'm sick of loving a man who sees right through me."

"Who are you in love with?" Jasper asked with a scowl.

"I've been in love with you for years, you blind fool!" Hazel shouted. Jasper's eyes bulged, and he began to stammer nonsensically.

Hazel snorted. "Although for the life of me I can't see why."

Misty Dingle let out a loud snort. "When are you men going to realize that loving someone means accepting their imperfections?"

"Absolutely!" Wanda shouted out. "You're far from perfect, Sheriff Prescott. And you, too, Gunther!"

"Me? What did I do?" Gunther asked, appearing dumbfounded as Wanda glared at him from across the table they shared.

"She made a mistake," Sophie cried from behind the counter, dabbing at her eyes with a tissue. "She's human. And she's a wonderful, caring person. She's incredibly loyal. More than you can even imagine."

For the first time Boone noticed Honor standing by the kitchen doorway taking it all in. She had a Moose T-shirt on, and her eyes were moist with unshed tears. Her expression begged him to reconsider his position. The look on her face said everything without her uttering a single word. He'd made a promise to her. Less judgment and more acceptance. Walking with love in his heart instead of censure. He knew she might lose faith in him forever if he didn't budge. But would his pride allow him to forgive Grace's deception? Could he swallow his anger long enough to reach out to her?

"Boone. It's not too late to work things out," Honor cried out. "Declan can get you to Anchorage in no time. And if you love Grace, letting her go isn't an option. If you do, it will hang over your head for the rest of your life."

Grace. Lovable, beautiful Gracie. Loving her hadn't been a choice. It had swept over him like a force of nature. From the very first moment they met, his heart had no longer been his own.

The last words he'd hurled at her had been full of judgment and anger. He'd been unyielding.

What had he done? He agonized. If he searched the world over, he would never find another woman like her. In a matter of weeks she'd worn down his defenses and nestled herself inside his hollow heart. She'd given him more happiness than he thought he'd ever experience in this lifetime. All those long, lonely nights when he'd stared out at the desolate sky, he'd asked the Lord to bring him a life partner. He'd prayed for someone to come along who could lift the fog away and make him care again. Someone who would make him cherish everything in his orbit.

Hadn't he received everything he'd prayed for when Gracie had crashed into his life?

Lord, give me the courage to face my fears. For so long I've been afraid to put my heart out there, at the risk of being made a fool of by love. I can't not love Gracie. She's everything I never thought I needed. But I do need her. Desperately. More than anything, I want to get to Grace, so I can tell her what's in my heart. Because the thought of losing her scares me more than anything in this world.

"Honor's right! I need to go get her. Before she leaves Alaska," Boone said, nodding his head in his sister's direction. Tears were freely running down her face. Upon hearing his words she laid her palm against her chest.

"That's the spirit, Boone!" Jasper cried out. "Halle-lujah!"

Hazel began clapping wildly. "Oh, Boone. Go sweep her off her feet."

"Are you ready to fly me to Anchorage?" Boone asked Declan.

"I was born ready," Declan drawled with a cocky nod of his head. He jumped up from his seat.

Boone rolled his eyes. Everyone within earshot let out a groan.

"Let's do this," Boone said as a burst of adrenaline roared through him. With Declan by his side he strode toward the exit, full of hope and anticipation and a small dose of fear.

"Boone," Cameron called out after him.

Boone turned around and met his brother's steady gaze. "Go get her and bring her back. Okay?"

He nodded at Cameron. "I'm prepared to do whatever it takes for a happily-ever-after." As he turned on his heel and left the Moose Café with his best friend right behind him, he could only pray that it wasn't too late.

Sitting in the Red Rooster coffee shop at the Anchorage airport felt like watching paint dry. Due to her last-minute ticket purchase, she now had to endure a six-hour layover. Only three hours had passed, yet it felt like forty. She'd sat down in the airport restaurant for a late breakfast, but every time she glanced at the menu her thoughts drifted back to Love. And the Moose Café. And all the people she'd disappointed. Especially Boone. All she could think about was the shattered look on his face when Dwight had exposed the truth. She'd never be able to get past the terrible way things had ended between them. It was far worse than being dumped at the altar. Because she loved Boone in a way she'd never loved anyone before in her life. And most likely never would again.

Somehow, Boone had plundered her heart like a swashbuckling pirate. He'd swooped in, knocked down all her defenses and stolen it right out from under her. With his generosity, sense of humor and kindness, he'd knocked down all her defenses. She loved him with a fierceness and a devotion she'd never imagined possible. And now, she would have to live with the fact that the man she loved couldn't stand the sight of her. And as much as she adored New York City, it was hard to wrap her head around going home when she'd already decided days ago that her future was in Love.

She'd slunk out of Love like a thief in the night. The thought of facing Jasper and Cameron and Hazel again had almost done her in. She didn't even want to think about seeing Boone again. It would gut her to have to listen once again to his recriminations. Saying goodbye to a sobbing Sophie had almost convinced her to stick around and plead her case to the man she loved. In the end, a part of her knew Boone deserved better than to have to deal with the fallout from all her lies.

Nothing about you is real. Pain ricocheted through her chest as Boone's devastating words ran through her mind. Not a single word he'd uttered had been untrue. She deserved his scorn, even though it destroyed her to know that he would always remember her as a liar and a fraud. And he would never know how much she loved him.

It no longer mattered. A quick glance at her watch told her it was time to head toward the security line so she could make her way toward the passengers' lounge.

"Gracie!" The sound of her name being called out in

a deep, urgent tone had her questioning her sanity. She looked up and found the last person she ever would have expected to see standing in front of her. Boone was there, intensity hovering over him like a cloud.

Confusion swirled around her. "Boone. What are you doing here?"

"I came for you, Gracie."

"For me?" Her voice came out sounding like a squeak.

He nodded his head. "Yes. For you."

Boone didn't look so steady at the moment despite the strong sentiment he'd voiced.

"You're...green," she said, noticing his face had an olive cast to it.

He squinted at her. "I'm what?"

"Your face is a little green."

He placed his hand over his stomach. "I'm a little queasy. Declan hit a few rough patches on the flight here. He flew straight through without changing his flight path to avoid turbulence. We knew we didn't have a moment to spare."

"I—I don't understand, Boone. What are you talking about?"

She watched as he inhaled a deep breath. "I manned up and faced my fears. Because of you."

"Me?" Grace furrowed her brow.

"Completely, absolutely, one-hundred percent because of you. I've been so wary of being betrayed again...after what happened in the past. I had one foot in our relationship and one foot out. Truthfully, I think I was waiting for the whole thing to blow up in my face."

"Because of the past?"

"Yes. And because the thought of losing you was overwhelming to me," Boone admitted.

"I thought you hated me." She felt her limbs trembling. "You said that you never wanted to see me again."

Boone reached out and grazed his thumb across her cheek. His eyes were filled with a tenderness and conviction she couldn't ignore.

"I was angry. Even though I've been walking toward my future ever since you came to Love, I took a giant step backward when I found out the reason you came to Alaska. It felt like a betrayal of everything we'd been building together. I had to question whether you were using me for a story. I allowed myself to get swallowed up by old hurts." He stared deeply into her eyes. "I'm ashamed of the things I said to you." He shuddered. "It makes me sick to my stomach just remembering how hard I was on you."

"You didn't say anything I didn't deserve to hear. I wasn't honest with you, Boone. I know how much you value the truth," she protested. "I should have been straight with you about everything right from the beginning."

He ran his fingers across her lips, gently tracing the outline of them. "You are the truth, Gracie. My truth. My love. I don't want you to go back to New York. Ever since you stepped off that seaplane and straight into my arms, Love has felt like a different place. Everywhere you go, you bring light and joy and an abundance of laughter. And even though you've struggled with your faith, you're working toward rebuilding your relationship with God. Brick by brick you're laying the foundation. We need you. I need you.

"I've fallen in love with you, Gracie. When I close my eyes and imagine my future, you're standing right there next to me. As my partner. My friend. My once-in-a-lifetime love. I love you, sweetheart."

Grace bowed her head. Tears sprung to her eyes and she blinked them away. This was the moment she'd prayed about for years. She'd asked God to bring her a faithful man who would love her until they both took their last breaths. She thought she'd lost Boone, but here he was with his heart in his hands, offering her the moon, sun and the stars. He loved her.

She inhaled a shaky breath. "I came to Alaska in search of a story, but I found so much more than I ever imagined. I found the love of my life in you, Boone. Above all else, I need you to know that."

Boone lowered his head and placed a tender kiss on her lips that was filled with emotion. "Hearing you say that you love me humbles me. That's all I'll ever need to know, Gracie. With love, all things are possible."

"And I don't blame you for being upset with me. I was here under false pretenses, and I feel terrible about hurting you and Jasper and Hazel. And everyone else who believed in me. From the beginning, everyone in Love welcomed me with open arms." She shut her eyes tight as a feeling of shame washed over her. When she opened them her lashes were awash in tears. "For the first time in my life, I felt like I was part of a community. It changed me, Boone. It made me a better person than the one who walked off that seaplane in pursuit of a story."

Boone took her in his arms and pressed a kissed on her forehead. "Part of loving someone includes forgiveness. What you brought to Love and to me—kindness, generosity, charm, goodness—those things are priceless. Not to mention your idea about making a business out of Hazel's boots. You've given us hope. A shot of adrenaline."

She grinned, feeling euphoric that Boone had said those three monumental words to her. And she'd finally been able to confess her love to him, as well. A few weeks ago she hadn't believed in the power behind those words. But now they meant the world to her because she knew Boone wouldn't throw them out casually.

The sheriff of Love was in love with her! *Yeah! Yeah! Yeah!*

"I love you so much, Boone." She reached up and placed her hands on either side of his face, drawing him down toward her so she could place a lingering kiss on his lips.

Boone let out a huff of air and placed his hand over his heart. "Hallelujah! If you didn't love me back, I wasn't sure what I was going to do. Maybe head back to Love with my tail between my legs or move to New York City and try to win your love."

"Maybe I should have held out a bit longer, just so I could see you roaming around New York," Grace teased.

She turned her head in the direction of a loud coughing sound. Declan was standing off to the side, wildly trying to get Boone's attention. He made an exaggerated motion with his hands and pointed toward the floor. Grace giggled at the sight of him. By the time she'd turned back toward Boone, he was down on bended knee.

She immediately stopped laughing. Boone was looking up at her with such a look of devotion it made her weak in the knees. A crowd had gathered nearby. People were looking and pointing. For this moment, all she wanted to do was focus on the man she loved. Grace wanted to remember this act of love for the rest of her years. She wanted to imprint every last detail on her soul so she could someday relay it to their children.

"Gracie, we met in the most unlikely of circumstances. You came to Alaska looking for a story. I told myself I wasn't looking for love, but deep down inside I yearned for it. I never expected to be bowled over by a city girl in four-inch heels. I am so deeply in love with you I can barely think straight. I can't for the life of me imagine my life without you in it."

Grace couldn't hold back the tears now. She was sniffling and choking back the sobs. Tears were coursing down her cheeks. She swiped them away with the back of her hand.

"So, Gracie, if you would do me the honor of becoming my wife, I vow to never let you regret it for a single, solitary moment."

She leaned down and wrapped her arms around his neck, showering him with kisses. "Yes, Boone. I'll marry you. I can't imagine a better life than one we can share together."

Tears welled in Boone's eyes. "I don't have a ring on me, but I do have this." He reached into his pocket and pulled out his sheriff's badge. "Not many things in this world mean more to me than this badge. It represents truth and dedication and commitment. All the things I intend to give you, Gracie. For the rest of our lives."

Boone stood up and pinned the badge on Grace's shirt, causing her to smile so wide she feared her face might crack. She ran her hand over the shiny star. It served as living proof of the principles they would build their lives around and of the strength of their love.

For now, and always, she would be the sheriff of Love's lady.

"Thanks for coming after me, Boone," she whispered. "It's the loveliest thing anyone has ever done for me."

"Oh, Gracie," he said with a sigh. "It was never really a choice. A life lived without you isn't really a life at all. At least not for me."

Grace stood on her tiptoes and placed an emotional kiss on Boone's lips. He was a keeper. *Thank You, Lord. For answering my prayers and pointing me in the direction of this wonderful man.*

"Let's go home, Boone," she murmured, knowing that from this moment forward they would be walking in love.

Epilogue

New York Tribune
Weddings

Grace Corbett of New York City was married today to Sheriff Boone Prescott in Love, Alaska. Grace, a journalist for the Tribune, *met Mr. Prescott while on assignment for the paper. Her popular series, "Finding Love in Alaska," details her courtship with her now husband. The couple plan to honeymoon in Hawaii and will reside in Love, Alaska, with their malamute, Kona.*

Grace nestled against Boone as they sat on their couch while her husband read the wedding announcement out loud to her. Kona was sitting at their feet, curled up in a ball. Grace was still dressed in her elegant vintage wedding dress with the faux fur collar and rhinestones on the bodice. Her ivory shoes, bejeweled with brilliant crystals, sat prettily on the hardwood floor. Boone, looking dashing in a black tuxedo, smiled down at her as he closed the computer and placed it back on the coffee table.

Their wedding this morning had been conducted by Pastor Jack in the presence of family, friends and an abundance of love. Sophie, Honor and Hazel had stood up as Grace's bridesmaids, with Liam, Declan and Cameron acting as Boone's groomsmen. Aidan, decked out in a little black suit, had marched down the aisle as the ring bearer. Grace brought Jasper to tears by asking him to walk her down the aisle. There hadn't been a dry eye in the chapel as they recited their wedding vows with both of them adding their own heartfelt words of commitment and devotion. In the morning they'd be flying to Anchorage to catch their flight to Oahu for ten days of paradise.

"The *Tribune* promised to send me a copy of the print edition. I can't wait to have it framed so I can put it in a place of honor," Grace said with a smile.

Boone leaned down and pressed a kiss on her forehead. "I can't wait to see our future unfold."

Grace reached up and placed a kiss on his cheek. "You're not the only one, Sheriff Prescott."

Boone gazed at her lovingly. "Any regrets about hanging up your hat at the *Tribune*?"

"Not a single one." Grace let out a contented sigh. "I'm right where I should be. And I can submit articles as a freelance journalist whenever I want, not to mention there are a few things I want to submit to other papers here in Alaska." She grabbed Boone's arm. "How does this sound? How to Survive in the Alaskan Wilderness. Alaskan Spelunking 101. Or how about this... Finding the Man of Your Dreams in Love, Alaska."

"I like the last one, especially since you're the woman of my dreams, Grace Prescott."

"Grace Prescott," she said in a dreamy voice. "I like

the way that sounds. It has a certain ring to it, don't you think?"

Boone brushed his lips across Grace's, his kiss full of tenderness and emotion.

"I think God blessed both of us the day He sent you to Love. Right from the beginning He gave us a sign when you fell right into my arms."

"Now I know what prayer He answered. I found everything I've always wanted right here in Love. Right here in your arms, Boone," Grace whispered, her voice husky with emotion. "I've always wanted a tight-knit family. Now I get to share yours."

"I'm not sure I want to share you with anybody just yet," Boone teased. "After all, we've barely been married a few hours. I like having you all to myself."

Grace giggled. "Jasper sure is tickled that we're the first couple to be married as a result of Operation Love."

"Something tells me we won't be the last. There are a lot of people who need love in this town," Boone drawled.

"Oh, Boone. We should help them. We could become the official ambassadors of Operation Love." Her voice rang out with enthusiasm. She tapped her finger alongside her jaw. "Imagine all the possibilities."

"That sounds a lot like matchmaking," Boone said with a raised eyebrow.

"It wouldn't really be matchmaking. Just giving the people we love a push in the right direction. Think about it. There's Cameron, Declan and Sophie. And of course there's Liam. And Honor."

Boone let out a groan. "Why can't you just be happy about Jasper and Hazel? Our wedding was their first official date. I haven't seen Jasper look so delighted in years."

"Oh, Sheriff Prescott, I am happy. Deliriously, ecstatically happy that I walked down the aisle toward the man I love. A man who greeted me at the altar with tenderness and joy and enthusiasm. Not to mention forgiveness. And with promises of a future to be lived out in love. I couldn't be more blessed."

"We couldn't be more blessed," Boone said as their lips met in a wonderful celebration of what they'd found in one another and everything the future held in store for them.

* * * * *

Dear Reader,

Thank you for joining me on this Alaskan adventure. I hope you enjoyed reading *An Alaskan Wedding*. Writing this book was a wonderful experience. It allowed me to inject a little humor into my work, which is always a treat. Alaska is such an exciting setting for a love story. Northern lights. Moose crossings. Frozen tundra. Good-looking bachelors! What's not to love?

Grace and Boone are perfect for one another in that both characters have a hole inside them that needs to be filled up. Boone isn't expecting a woman like Grace to crash into his life in such a meaningful way. Grace is so focused on her career as a journalist that the last thing she wants is to fall in love. Meeting and falling for Boone, as well as the residents of Love, is a priceless gift. In Alaska she finds a soft place to fall and people who treasure her, imperfections and all. And after taking care of his siblings for so many years, Boone deserves his own happily-ever-after with Grace.

Finding a place to call home is a universal theme. Who doesn't want to be loved and protected and sheltered from the storms of life? I truly feel fortunate to have met my husband when we were in college. Whether we're watching a movie together at home or going out on the town, I always feel as if I'm safe, protected and deeply loved. My prayer is that each of you has a place to call home filled with love, happiness and a soft place to fall.

As always, writing for the Love Inspired line is an honor. I feel very blessed to have my dream job.

I love hearing from readers, however you choose to

contact me. You can reach me by email at scalhoune@gmail.com, at my Author Belle Calhoune Facebook page or at my website, bellecalhoune.com. If you're on Twitter, reach out to me, @BelleCalhoune.

Blessings,
Belle